ORCHARD BOOKS
First published in Great Britain in 2018 by The Watts Publishing Group

1 3 5 7 9 10 8 6 4 2

Text copyright © Christopher William Hill, 2018
Cover and inside illustrations by David Litchfield copyright © Orchard Books, 2018

The moral rights of the author and illustrator have been asserted.

A CIP catalogue record for this book
is available from the British Library.

ISBN 978 1 40833 293 1

Printed and bound in Great Britain by CIP Group (UK) Ltd, Croydon, CRO 4YY

The paper and board used in this book are from well-managed forests and other
responsible sources.

Orchard Books
An imprint of
Hachette Children's Group
Part of The Watts Publishing Group Limited
Carmelite House
50 Victoria Embankment
London EC4Y 0DZ

An Hachette UK Company
www.hachette.co.uk

www.hachettechildrens.co.uk

WHAT MANOR OF MURDER?

A BLEAKLEY BROTHERS MYSTERY

by
Christopher William Hill

ORCHARD

For Emma Spurgin Hussey

(if that really is her name)

Michaelmas daisies among wild weeds
Bloom for St Michael's valiant deeds
You slayed a dragon, killed it dead
Now save us from Old Bramble Head!

Chapter One

The Curse of Old Bramble Head

'THE TROUBLE WITH mysteries is this,' said Horatio Bleakley, pulling the sucked remains of an aniseed ball from his mouth so he could make his point more clearly, 'the harder you wish for something rippingly exciting to happen, the less likely it is that anything will happen at all. Umbrellas work in much the same way; there's always more chance of rain if you *don't* take your umbrella than if you do.'

It was late September and the Bleakley brothers were travelling by motorcar to the home of their aunt and uncle for the Michaelmas weekend. They were warmly wrapped up in long overcoats and scarves and each wore his striped school cap. Outside the sky was leaden and a driving rain battered against the windows of the car.

'It's all well and good you saying that,' replied Eustace Bleakley patiently, 'but if a fellow isn't paying proper attention to what's going on around him, then half a dozen mysteries could whizz past undetected. Let's not forget how I solved the mystery of Piggy Paterson's disappearing chocolate biscuits.'

'They were only disappearing because Piggy was eating them,' snorted Horatio.

'Yes, but in his *sleep*,' protested Eustace. 'It took an ingenious bit of detective work to hit upon that solution.'

'Solution?' laughed Horatio, rolling his eyes. 'Piggy woke up every morning surrounded by biscuit crumbs. Even the most pudding-headed nincompoop could have solved *that* puzzle!'

It was clear they were not destined to agree, so Eustace helped himself to an aniseed ball, sank back in his seat and considered the best way to make a mystery happen, even if a mystery showed no sign of wanting to happen.

Eustace was rather taller for his age than was quite usual, and this he attributed to superior intelligence and a reluctance to play sports. He had a long face and brown hair, entirely straight save for a cowlick at the fringe which interrupted the uniformity of his face and which he was at constant pains to tame. Horatio, three minutes younger and three inches shorter than his brother, was a sturdy boy with untidy hair who prized sports above studies. Though the brothers were separated in age by no more than one hundred and eighty seconds, Eustace was known at school as Bleakley Major (a title in which he revelled) and Horatio, Bleakley Minor (a title which he loathed).

It was tradition that the far-flung members of the family should descend on Bleakley Manor once a year at Michaelmas-tide, and as Eustace had done well in his Latin exams, the boys' parents had arranged for a chauffeur in a gleaming black motorcar to collect them from boarding school.

As the car raced along the narrow country lanes,

splashing through deep puddles, a thought occurred to Eustace and he slipped an envelope from his blazer pocket. He removed a folded sheet of mauve writing paper, headed with the Bleakley family crest of two black crows above crossed swords.

Bleakley Manor
Ludd-on-Lye
Fenshire

Eustace and Horatio,

Your father has sent a telegram to inform me that you will be arriving on the 28th of September by motorcar from your school. Why he has run to the expense of hiring such a vehicle I really cannot say, but I imagine there must be a reason for it. Whatever reason that might be is of no consequence, but I would be grateful if you would stop at the railway station at Brockton Mannerley at 3 o'clock to collect Master Oliver Davenport, who will also be staying with us for the Michaelmas weekend. Master Davenport is a _Poor Unfortunate_ and we must take pity on the boy, no matter how inconvenient that may be.

Please be certain not to bring any unnecessary dirt to the house.

Aunt Maude

'Is Master Oliver Davenport an orphan, do you think?' asked Horatio, as Eustace refolded the letter and returned it to his pocket.

'I'm rather afraid he is,' said Eustace. 'Aunt Maude generally means "orphan" when she writes "Poor Unfortunate" with capital letters.' Leaning forward, he wound down the connecting window to speak to the chauffeur. 'Don't forget we're collecting Master Oliver Davenport from the railway station. It isn't very far out of our way.'

'Very good, sir,' said the chauffeur.

The down train had just departed from Brockton Mannerley as the car arrived, and a billowing cloud of white steam hung heavy above the station buildings. A small boy with a shock of curly red hair was waiting patiently outside in the rain, surrounded

13

by an assortment of bags and battered suitcases. Eustace and Horatio climbed out of the motorcar to greet the new arrival.

Eustace walked ahead, as seemed right and proper for a boy three minutes his brother's senior. 'You must be Master Oliver Davenport,' he called, opening out an umbrella. 'I'm Bleakley Major and this is my brother, Bleakley Minor.'

'We're not at school now,' tutted Horatio. 'We only need our first names.' He smiled at the newcomer. 'I'm Horatio and this blighter is my brother, Eustace.'

'Hullo. Very pleased to meet you,' said Master Oliver Davenport, all the time jabbing vigorously at his right eye with the corner of a grubby pocket handkerchief. 'I would shake hands, you know, only I got a smut in my eye and it's absolute agony.'

'Were you leaning out of the compartment window?' asked Horatio.

'I was,' said the boy.

'You would have had your head sliced off if there'd been a train coming in the other direction,' said

14

Horatio cheerfully. 'Heaps of boys have had their heads hacked off by passing steam trains. They're always warning us of it at school.'

'At least my eye wouldn't be hurting if my head *had* come off,' said Master Oliver Davenport philosophically, prodding his eye again with the grimy handkerchief. 'There, I think that's shifted it.'

The rain was falling heavily now and the chauffeur took care of Master Oliver Davenport's luggage as the boys climbed gratefully into the warm motorcar, slamming the doors shut behind them.

'Have you had to travel very far from your school?' asked Eustace, as the engine hummed once more and the car pulled slowly away from the station.

'Two hours and three trains,' replied Master Oliver Davenport. 'The more distance there is between me and those tormentors of souls who pass themselves off as teachers, the better.' He grinned at the two boys. 'It seems your family has taken pity on me. Are they frightfully rich, your aunt and uncle?'

Eustace considered it poor form to discuss

the wealth of his relatives. But as Master Oliver Davenport was shortly to arrive at Bleakley Manor and the enormous wealth of the family would become manifestly obvious, he broke his golden rule. 'Absolutely rolling in cash,' he said. 'Oodles of the stuff. Uncle Max is chairman of Bleakley Bottling Inc. – they make pickles, you know.'

'Cripes,' said Master Oliver Davenport, his eyes wide with surprise. 'We have their mustard piccalilli in our sandwiches at school. But very thinly spread, more's the pity.'

'It's the mustard piccalilli that made the Bleakley fortune,' said Eustace. 'The family hardly had a penny in the bank before Uncle Max took up pickling. Bleakley Manor was practically falling down around his ears.'

Master Oliver Davenport smiled. 'Just the sort of rich old cove who gets bumped off in a ripping murder mystery. You know, with some treacherous relative hoping to get their hands on the loot.' He proffered a paper bag. 'Peanut brittle?'

Eustace and Horatio each took a nugget of the peanut brittle and settled back in their seats, gazing out of the windows as the flat, waterlogged landscape flashed past.

'Did your aunt describe me as a Poor Unfortunate?' asked Master Oliver Davenport. 'That's how I'm generally introduced into conversations.'

Though Master Oliver Davenport had been described in precisely those terms, Eustace and Horatio were polite enough not to admit it.

'I'm an orphan, you see,' added the boy by way of explanation, sucking so hard on a shard of the peanut brittle that his tongue throbbed.

'Yes, dashed hard luck,' murmured Horatio.

'It's not so bad, really,' continued Master Oliver Davenport. 'My parents were frightfully well-connected before they kicked the bucket. And now all sorts of people take pity on me and invite me to stay. It gives them a tremendous thrill having a needy orphan about the place … good Samaritans and all that.' He turned hopefully to his fellow passengers. 'I don't suppose you're orphans as well, are you? Is that why you're staying with your aunt and uncle?'

Eustace shook his head. 'No, our parents are still very much alive,' he replied apologetically. 'They live in India.'

'Of course they *could* be dead by now,' said Horatio, not wishing to appear boastful about the fortunate survival of their own mother and father. 'Lots of tigers and snakes and things. And it takes such a long time to wire through a telegram. They might have been dead for weeks and weeks and we'd both be none the wiser.'

'It's kind of you to say so,' said Master Oliver Davenport. 'But if they haven't been eaten by tigers, what is it they do in India?'

'Father is a diplomat,' said Eustace.

'And Mother is something to do with cocktail parties,' added Horatio as the car roared on towards Ludd-on-Lye. 'I forget what.'

'When we're not at boarding school we have our hols with Aunt Amelia and Cousin Loveday,' said

Eustace. 'And every year at Michaelmas the family gathers at Bleakley Manor.'

'Whether we like it or not,' said Horatio, with a wink to his brother. 'We never have worked out if it's a treat or a punishment.'

A thought seemed to dawn on Master Oliver Davenport. 'I hope you won't think me too inquisitive for asking,' he said, pulling out a rolled-up copy of *The Archaeological Gazette* from his blazer pocket, 'but is this Bleakley a relative of yours?' He leafed quickly through the pages of the magazine and pointed to a photograph of an explorer in long shorts and a pith helmet. The man was standing at the entrance to an unearthed tomb, leaning against a large terracotta bust engraved with ancient Egyptian hieroglyphs.

Horatio laughed. 'He's one of our uncles,' he said. 'Colonel Theodore Bleakley. Always digging things up halfway across the world. A priceless chap but nutty as a fruitcake. He'd be just as happy with an old cracked pot as he would with a treasure chest full of gold.'

'He's a bit of a hero of mine actually,' confessed Master Oliver Davenport. 'I've read all about his exploits in Egypt. He was trying to uncover the treasure of Arn Akh.'

'And what treasure was that?' asked Eustace, who had lost track of his uncle's failed searches for lost riches.

'A solid gold statue of Osiris, the Egyptian god of the afterlife,' replied Master Oliver Davenport. He tapped the pages of the magazine. 'It was thought to have been hidden inside a terracotta bust, but it was never found. It's worth a King's ransom. You should read the article. It's a corking story, even if the Colonel did come back empty-handed.'

'When he's not off exploring, he lives at Bleakley Manor,' said Eustace. 'He'll be there for Michaelmas, you can count on that.'

'I was awfully bucked to be coming back with you for the weekend anyway,' gushed Master Oliver Davenport. 'But if Colonel Theodore Bleakley's going to be there as well … cripes, that's the icing on the cake!'

The motorcar turned a sharp corner that brought them into the village of Ludd-on-Lye. It was a bleak place of grey stone and ancient wooden beams. A fast-running stream, fed by the downpour, gurgled along by the side of the road. As the car passed a small parade of shops, Eustace opened the connecting window once more to speak to the chauffeur.

'There's a newsagent's on the left-hand side up ahead,' said the boy, who wished to buy pencils and a new pocket notebook in the fervent hope that a mystery might occur, no matter what Horatio said to the contrary. 'Would you stop there, please?'

'Yes, sir. Very good, sir,' said the chauffeur, applying the brakes and pulling up alongside the shop.

As Eustace stocked up on stationery, Horatio and Master Oliver Davenport chose sweets from the long row of glass jars behind the shop counter. The boys made their selection with infinite care, deciding between peppermint bulls-eyes and pineapple cubes;

liquorice toffees and buttered brazils.

'We'll have a quarter of the liquorice toffees, please,' said Master Oliver Davenport at last.

The young woman serving took down the jar and emptied the sweets on to the scales. 'Just over the quarter,' she said.

Master Oliver Davenport smiled greedily. 'I'd rather have it over than under.'

'You're Sir Max and Lady Maude's nephews, aren't you?' said the woman, scooping the toffees into a paper bag.

'That's right,' replied Horatio. 'And this is a new friend of ours, Master Oliver Davenport. We're staying at Bleakley Manor for the Michaelmas weekend.'

A hacking cough and a cloud of tobacco smoke announced the arrival of a hunched and elderly man from the back room of the shop. 'What's that you say?' he asked, sucking on an old briar pipe. 'Bleakley Manor, is it? Careful Old Bramble Head don't come an' get you, that's what I says.'

'What do you mean?' asked Master Oliver Davenport, shooting an anxious glance at Horatio. 'Who's Old Bramble Head?'

'We know the legend all right, sir,' laughed Horatio. 'But I think we'll be safe enough at the manor for another year.'

The old man fixed the boys with piercing grey eyes and sucked again on his pipe. 'That's what you think, is it?' he rasped, leaning against the counter and breathing out a thick fog of smoke. 'Well, let me tell you this much, my lad—'

'Enough of your nonsense, Granfer,' chided the young woman. 'You're scaring the boys.' She turned to Eustace and smiled nervously. 'I've got more notebooks out the back,' she said. 'I'll go and fetch them for you.'

As the woman hurried away the old man leaned across the shop counter, lowering his voice so he could not be overheard by his granddaughter. 'There's dark things at Bleakley Manor,' he said. 'Things that certain folk don't want me a-telling of to the likes of you.'

'The likes of us?' repeated Eustace. 'Whatever do you mean?'

'Young 'uns, I means,' explained the old man. 'Impressionable minds that'll get the horrors if I tells 'em all the dark tales I knows of.'

'It's all just superstition,' said Horatio. 'There's not a word of truth in it.'

But the old man shook his head. 'Old Bramble Head will rise up come midnight on Michaelmas Eve, you mark my words,' he hissed. 'With shoulders wreathed in brambles and his wicked grin stained dark with blackberries.'

Master Oliver Davenport shivered, as though an icy hand had passed slowly along his spine. 'But that's tonight,' he whispered hoarsely.

There was no stopping the old man now his tale was begun. 'Arms like pitchforks, he's got,' he continued, slowly raising his hands and extending his long, bony fingers. 'His bramble claws *scratch scratch* at the windowpanes. And his face ...' He shook his head and moaned in horror. 'Such a terrible face! It's not skin as you might think, but more alike to sackcloth than human flesh. His breath is of the marsh. There's no hair to speak of; instead the creature's all over brambles. And when he catches his victims, he drags 'em down to their deaths in the marsh water, never to be seen ag—'

'Granfer!' snapped the woman, returning from the back room with the notebooks. 'That's enough!'

The old man scowled at his granddaughter and turned away from the boys. Reaching up to a shelf for a tin of condensed milk, he shuffled out the way he had come, lost in another choking cloud of tobacco smoke.

Eustace selected a pocket notebook with a red cover. The boys paid for their supplies and made their way to the door,

'And a happy Michaelmas to you all,' said the young woman, though her voice seemed to tremble as she spoke and the words struck hollow.

The boys stepped outside on to the pavement and the shop bell jangled noisily behind them.

'How peculiar,' said Master Oliver Davenport, with a nervous laugh. 'I half-believed the old man when he started talking about Old Bramble Head.'

'It's not all that peculiar,' said Horatio, helping himself to a liquorice toffee. 'Not in these parts, at any rate. Ludd-on-Lye is a strange place.'

'They are rather prone to superstition,' agreed Eustace, as they crossed the pavement and climbed back into the waiting motorcar. 'It's an old myth that Bleakley Manor is haunted by a creature from the marshes. They say it was a servant who was turned mad by the marsh vapours several centuries ago and came back transformed into a monster to wreak his revenge on the Bleakley family. But it's all stuff and nonsense, of course.'

The car roared past the Stoat and Raven pub before passing the old stone pillar that marked the boundary between the village and the outer fringes of the Bleakley estate.

'That's the manor house in the distance,' said Eustace, sitting up in his seat and pointing ahead.

'You can just about see the chimney pots through the trees.'

The house was reached by way of an ancient road bridge on wooden struts across a wide expanse of green marshland. The chauffeur slowed the motorcar to a crawl and drove cautiously over the creaking bridge. Horatio wound down his window and leaned out so that he had an uninterrupted view across the marshes.

'What would happen if the bridge were to fall down?' asked Master Oliver Davenport, hardly daring to glance out as the car rolled slowly over the rickety planks.

'Then Bleakley Manor would be cut off from Ludd-on-Lye,' said Horatio. 'It's an island really. When it's as wet as this, there's no way of crossing the marsh without being sucked down to your certain doom.'

Master Oliver Davenport shuddered and screwed his eyes shut.

At the end of the bridge, a gravel path snaked

through a dark tunnel of horse chestnut trees on its approach to the house. As the car rounded a corner, the wind picked up and the boys were greeted by an ominous howl of foreboding. High above them, standing out in sharp relief against the slate-grey sky, loomed the towering walls of Bleakley Manor.

Chapter Two

A Stranger at the Door

THE MOTORCAR CAME to a crunching halt on the gravel and the chauffeur climbed out to help the three boys with their luggage. Though the rain had eased, the sky was dark and brooding. A howling wind rocked the horse chestnut trees and crows chattered uneasily from the branches. 'So, this where you're staying for your Michaelmas weekend, is it?' asked the man.

'That's right,' said Eustace. 'Bleakley Manor. The family pile.'

'Gives me the shivers just looking at it,' said the chauffeur, glancing up at the house. It was a strange, lofty building of red brick, with tall and slender chimneys the shape of barley sugar twists. 'Like something out of the horror flicks.'

As the boys took their bags and cases from the boot of the motorcar, a taxi cab drew up behind them.

'Look!' cried Horatio as a girl inside the cab waved violently at the boys. 'It's Cousin Loveday!'

'Hello, cuz,' said Eustace as the taxi stopped and Loveday jumped out, slamming the door so hard behind her that the boys were quite certain it would snap off at the hinges.

'I wanted him to race you,' said Loveday with a grin. 'But he wouldn't. Not an ounce of sporting spirit in him!' She was a thin and gangly girl, with a rash of freckles and hair tied up in messy pigtails. In one hand she clutched a suitcase and in the other a badly battered lacrosse stick.

'I thought Aunt Amelia was coming with you?' said Horatio.

'Oh, you know what Muv's like,' huffed Loveday. 'She had another of her swooning fits and she packed me off on my own. If you ask me, she's using it as an excuse to wriggle out of the festivities, and who can blame the old pet? Now my back's turned she's most likely stretched out in front of the gramophone scoffing chocolates by the boxful. So, who's the new inmate?' She smiled at the newcomer and gave the boy a jovial prod on the shoulder with the tip of her lacrosse stick. 'Staying for Michaelmas, are you?'

'This is Master Oliver Davenport,' said Horatio. 'He's an orphan.'

'Pleased to meet you,' said Loveday. 'Actually, my father snuffed it before I was born so I suppose I'm a half-orphan.'

'That doesn't really count,' said Master Oliver Davenport. 'But you're very kind to make the effort.'

The motorcar and the taxi cab roared off along the drive, disappearing behind the tall trees, and the four children were left alone.

'At last,' said Loveday with a deep sigh of relief. 'Free from Miss Sunnybrook's School for a whole weekend!'

Master Oliver Davenport stood gazing up at the lofty brick walls of Bleakley Manor. 'It's not a nice house,' said Eustace, as if reading the boy's mind. 'But it's a solid house. It's not likely to crumble to dust while we're asleep in our beds.'

'It looks like the sort of place where bad things have happened,' whispered Master Oliver Davenport.

Loveday and her cousins knew well the grim history of the great house. It had begun its existence modestly enough but had swollen over the centuries, becoming progressively uglier with each passing generation of the Bleakley family. It had grown up and it had grown out; a turret had been added here, a parapet there. The entire edifice was wrapped round with ivy, as if held together by an enormous green sticking plaster.

'Oh, heaps and heaps of bad things,' said Loveday, tearing at the ivy with her lacrosse stick and sending a cluster of spiders scuttling for cover.

'Well, here we are,' said Eustace, as they climbed the stone steps to the house.

Master Oliver Davenport peered up at the vast door of studded oak that was the port of entry to Bleakley Manor, flinching as a crow cackled at him from the parapet. Above the door was a stone carving of the family crest. He attempted to make out the wording, which had been worn and pitted by centuries of inclement weather. '*Mors cum* … ?'

'*Mors cum laetitia*,' finished Eustace. 'It's the family motto. It means "death with joyfulness".'

'Not the jolliest of mottos, I suppose,' said Loveday. 'But then, the Bleakleys aren't the jolliest of families.'

Eustace reached up and pulled at a heavy iron handle beside the door. Master Oliver Davenport jumped as a bell rang out from the deepest depths of the house.

'I can't wait to see old Watkins again,' said Horatio. 'He's been with the family for an age,' he explained. 'Practically since time began. He's always ripe for japes and wheezes … magic tricks and all sorts of things. Aunt Maude and Uncle Max absolutely depend on him … he's the only sane fellow in the nuthouse.'

The door creaked open and Eustace, Horatio and Loveday smiled expectantly. But the face that peered back from behind the ancient door was not the face they were expecting. It was a butler, of that there was no doubt, but not the revered Watkins. The man had a long, lozenge-shaped face and his hair had been neatly oiled with pomade.

'You rang?' intoned the butler.

Eustace was taken aback. 'We're expected,' he stammered. 'Eustace and Horatio Bleakley, Loveday Bleakley and Master Oliver Davenport.'

'Yes, Master Eustace,' said the butler, opening the door wide and bowing from the waist.

'We were rather expecting Watkins,' said Horatio, a look of disappointment etched on his face.

'So, who are *you*?' demanded Loveday.

'My name is Horton, Miss Loveday,' replied the butler as he led the young guests inside. 'I have been in Sir Max's employ for the past two months. I shall endeavour to make your stay here an enjoyable one.'

'Do you do magic tricks?' asked Horatio, hopefully.

'I do not,' replied the butler, with an apologetic bob of his head.

The grandfather clock in the hall chimed the quarter hour, a doleful noise that brought two enormous shaggy dogs clattering out into the passageway. Sighting the children, they gave enthusiastic howls of welcome and bounded on along the polished wooden floor. The larger of the two dogs rose up to rest its paws on Master Oliver Davenport's shoulders and the boy was almost knocked backwards.

'This is Mustard,' said Horatio, patting the smaller of the two dogs. 'And that's Pickle. They're Irish Wolfhounds.'

Pickle licked the side of Master Oliver Davenport's face, leaving behind a glistening trail of drool.

'They're hopeless,' laughed Loveday. 'Uncle Max bought them as guard dogs, but they're too fond of strangers to be any good at chasing off burglars.'

'Can you ride them?' asked Master Oliver Davenport, gently pushing Pickle away. 'I mean, like donkeys at the seaside?'

'Don't be an ass,' said Horatio.

Master Oliver Davenport glanced around the hall. The place was awash with taxidermy; there were cases of tropical birds on the walls, an elephant's foot umbrella stand with assorted canes and hunting sticks, and a large brown bear, badly moulted, which stood on its hind legs at the bottom of the great oak staircase holding a glass box for visiting cards. The boy shivered; wherever he looked, some exotic and long-dead creature was peering down at him through glassy eyes.

Horton gave a respectful cough. 'Shall I show you to your rooms, Master Eustace?'

'That's all right,' said Loveday, swinging her lacrosse stick cheerfully and striking the stuffed bear hard on the back of the head. 'I should jolly well hope we know our way by now. We've been coming here for Michaelmas since we were babes in arms.'

Horton reached out a hand to steady the tottering bear before it could fall and crush Master Oliver Davenport. 'If that will be all?' he said.

'You might send Herbert to carry up our luggage,' said Horatio. 'There is rather a lot of it.'

'Very good, Master Horatio,' said Horton. 'But it won't be Herbert, I am afraid. It will be Percival.'

Loveday blinked hard. 'Percival?' she echoed. 'Cripes! Don't tell me there's a new footman as well?'

'Indeed, Miss Loveday,' replied Horton. 'It is so difficult to keep staff these days.' With another bow of his head, he turned and disappeared along the dark passageway.

The children were not left alone for long. A door opened at the end of the hall and a tall and formidable woman appeared. Her hair was set in immaculate waves and she wore a string of pearls wound several times around her long neck. She seemed surprised to see the four children standing before her. 'Is it Michaelmas Eve already?' she asked vaguely.

'Hello, Aunt Maude,' said Eustace.

'Eustace, of course,' said Aunt Maude, seeming to gather her wits. 'And Loveday and Horatio.' Her gaze wandered and alighted on Master Oliver Davenport, who was standing patiently beside the stuffed bear, looking poorer and more unfortunate than ever. 'And you must be Master Oliver Davenport.'

Master Oliver Davenport nodded in confirmation that this was indeed the case.

'I knew your late mother,' said Aunt Maude. 'Millicent was one of my closest girlhood friends.'

Master Oliver Davenport gave an apologetic cough and raised his hand. 'But my mother's name was Gertrude,' he said.

Aunt Maude sighed. 'Please don't contradict, dear. Now, all of you, go up and change out of your school clothes at once. And do wash your hands. I simply will *not* have sticky finger marks on the furniture. Loveday, I've left a length of ribbon on your bed so you can do something about your hair.'

'How kind of you, Aunt Maude,' said Loveday through gritted teeth, as her aunt turned and walked away with the wolfhounds at her heels.

'She likes her guests to have neatly brushed hair and clean hands, but beyond that she isn't too fussy about things,' said Eustace, leading the way upstairs.

Horatio laughed. 'I don't think she'd even mind awfully if your arm dropped off at the dinner table – so long as it was a *clean* arm.'

At the top of the staircase a wide passageway led to the east wing of the house, where the children were to stay. The walls were lined with oil portraits of the Bleakley family, in ornate frames of cracked and crumbling gilt plaster.

'Are these all your ancestors?' asked Master Oliver Davenport, very much impressed.

'That's right,' said Loveday. 'And every one of them dead,' she added with relish, rolling the word 'dead' around in her mouth like a delicious bonbon.

Master Oliver Davenport was staring at a large painting of the Duke of Wellington leaning over a stricken Bleakley ancestor who lay on his back in a pool of mud.

'That was our Great Great Uncle Peregrine Bleakley,' said Horatio. 'He was a captain in the army.'

'Did he die at the Battle of Waterloo?' asked Master Oliver Davenport, who knew his history.

'On his *way* to Waterloo,' said Loveday. 'He slipped from the saddle and was trampled to death by his own horse.'

'A tragic end,' said Master Oliver Davenport solemnly.

'Not especially,' laughed Horatio. 'Unpleasant things have been happening to the Bleakley family more or less since the Norman Conquests.'

'Where are all your ancestors buried?' asked Master Oliver Davenport.

'They used to throw the bodies into the marshes,' explained Eustace. 'Only trouble was, the bodies had a habit of popping up again every now and then.'

'You're talking rot,' said Master Oliver Davenport with a smile, sensing that his leg was being pulled.

'No,' replied Eustace stiffly. 'I never make up a single thing. It's in the Bleakley Family Record, as a matter of fact.'

Horatio grinned darkly. 'And without dead bodies to feast on, Old Bramble Head would have deserted us years ago!'

Master Oliver Davenport gulped. Loveday laughed and gave Horatio a hard shove.

They carried on along the gallery corridor, passing bronze and plaster busts of long-ago ancestors, as the brothers continued their colourful commentary, detailing the many and varied ways in which each member of the Bleakley family had met his or her untimely end.

'Art's all very well and good, I suppose,' said Master Oliver Davenport at last, 'but will there be cake any time soon, do you think?'

'There's always cake,' said Horatio. 'If we buck up and dump our school togs, we can be downstairs in the kitchen in two jiffies. Cook's first rate when it comes to grub!'

With the prospect of cake cheering them on their way, the children climbed the staircase to the old nursery wing at the very top of the house.

'That's my room,' said Loveday to Master Oliver Davenport, pointing to a door at the far end of the dark and narrow corridor. 'I'll stow away my belongings and be back in a tick.' And with that she plodded off along the creaking floorboards, her lacrosse stick swung nonchalantly over her shoulder.

'This is our dorm,' said Horatio, turning a door handle and leading the way into the room. 'It's more like a gaol cell than a bedroom, but it's home for the weekend!'

Master Oliver Davenport stepped inside and gazed about him. It was a high-ceilinged room with three iron bedsteads standing on bare wooden floorboards. An old armchair that had split its seams stood in a corner of the room. The paint on the ceiling was peeling off in patches and the sash windows rattled in their frames as the wind and rain buffeted against the side of the house.

Eustace closed the door to shut out the draught. 'Not much to look at, is it?' he said, as disappointment flashed across Master Oliver

Davenport's face. 'We're never here for more than a few days each year, and Aunt Maude doesn't see the sense in squandering money on the old nursery wing to make it pleasant for children.'

'This is my bed,' said Horatio, swinging his case on to the bed that stood nearest the door. 'And that's Eustace's bed in the corner. That'll be yours, next to the washstand.'

'Are there mice, do you know?' asked Master Oliver Davenport, glancing anxiously beneath his bed.

'Tons of them,' said Horatio. 'And rats too. They feed on the mice.'

The door opened and a young footman backed into the room, dragging Master Oliver Davenport's bags and cases. He dropped the largest case heavily and the floorboards quivered from the shock. Turning, he was surprised to see the three boys staring at him.

'I didn't know you was up here,' said the footman. It was more an accusation than an apology.

Eustace observed the man closely. He wore an ill-fitting tailcoat and the tips of his fingers were yellow from cigarette smoke. Though he was no more than twenty-five, his face seemed set in a permanent scowl and he appeared older than his years. 'You must be Percy, the new footman.'

'Oh, must I?' muttered the man, scowling harder than ever. 'And I'll thank you to call me Percival. Shows the proper dignity of me position, don't it?'

'Quite right,' said Eustace quickly, not wishing to hurt the man's feelings. 'How long have you been here, Percival?'

'A month,' answered the footman with a sniff.

'Where were you before?' asked Horatio.

Percival cast his eyes to the floor and shuffled his feet. 'I was with Lord Crutchley.' He sniffed again, and looked up. 'Not that it's any of your business where I was, is it? You ain't the police, are you?'

'Well spotted,' said Horatio sarcastically. 'We're not.'

'Will that be all?' grunted Percival.

'Yes, thank you,' said Eustace.

The footman gave a cursory nod and departed.

Eustace pushed the door closed. 'Well, I don't think much of him,' he pronounced grimly, slipping out his pocket notebook and committing his thoughts to paper:

Percival, the new footman, a rotter, with a dark secret on his mind, perhaps?

Master Oliver Davenport pushed his bags and cases across the floor and stacked them carefully in a corner of the room.

'You can hardly blame him for being a little disgruntled,' said Horatio. 'His arms must have been stretched at least an inch or two dragging all those cases upstairs. You do have an awful lot of luggage. Just for one weekend, I mean.'

'We Poor Unfortunates tend to, as a rule,' said Master Oliver Davenport. 'We're pitched from pillar to post and have to cart round all our worldly goods wherever we go. We never know where we're going

to end up or what we might need when we get there.'
He sat heavily on his bed and the springs creaked
and groaned beneath him.

Horatio hung his school blazer in the wardrobe,
safely out of harm's way, and observed his roommate
with interest. He couldn't quite bring himself to
call the new friend 'Davenport' or 'Oliver'. The
boy seemed somehow incomplete without all three
names. So 'Master Oliver Davenport' it would for
ever more be.

Eustace opened a large chest of drawers and began
unpacking his case. He was methodical to the core;
his shirts had been precisely folded and his socks
were rolled into perfect spheres, the size of cricket
balls. He carefully stowed his collars and collar studs
in a leather box on top of the chest. Finally, he took
out a pair of striped flannel pyjamas, a copy of *The
Big Book of Crime* and a torch, all of which he tucked
away tidily beneath his pillow.

Horatio's clothes had been hastily thrust into his
case. Two shirts had become stuck together by a

stray toffee that had oozed from its wrapper and, in defiance of probability, not a single one of his socks had its pair.

Eustace combed his hair neatly in the mirror as Horatio sucked the toffee smear from one of the shirts.

The door creaked open and Loveday lolloped into the room, two large books in her hands. She flung herself into the armchair, sending silverfish scuttling from behind the cushions. 'Aunt Maude must think I've got porridge for brains,' she grunted. 'No books about motorcars or hand grenades. This is the rot she left me instead: *Luckley's Lazy Days for Little Ladies* and *The Sunny Days Book for Girls*. I've flicked through them both and there's not a single corpse to be seen.' She reached into her pocket and fished out a sheaf of crumpled papers, held together with a grubby length of string. 'Unlike this.'

'What've you got there?' asked Eustace.

'A new venture of mine,' said Loveday, sitting forward and thrusting the papers into her cousin's hands. '*Murder and Mayhem Magazine.* I'm editor-in-chief and head reporter.'

'What's it about?' asked Master Oliver Davenport.

'Bad things that have happened and bad things that might happen,' said Loveday. 'Some of the mayhem I've carried out myself,' she added proudly.

'Well, Eustace?' said Horatio impatiently. 'Let us in on it.'

Eustace frowned. 'The first story appears to be about a giant ferret in Yorkshire with a taste for blood.'

'They eat rabbits, don't they?' said Master Oliver Davenport. 'Ferrets?'

'Not in my story they don't,' grinned Loveday. 'My ferret feeds exclusively on schoolmistresses. I'll set the scene for you. It's a bright moonlit night and Miss Fairchild, the brutal new gym mistress, is pursued over open moorland by the monstrous bounding ferret—'

'Yes, I think that's enough of that,' interrupted Eustace, who knew that unless Cousin Loveday was stopped in her tracks the greater part of the day would be taken up with murderous ferrets.

'Ripping stuff though, isn't it?' said Loveday. 'I painted in the pools of blood myself!'

'It's rather gory,' said Horatio, reading over Eustace's shoulder.

'It has to be, idiot,' replied Loveday, snatching the pages back. 'It is called *Murder and Mayhem Magazine*. I write it and then Roberta Smith types it all up. She's a great·pal of mine. She has a portable typewriter, you see.'

'Is there only one copy then?' asked Eustace.

'Roberta's got a typewriter, not a printing press,' said Loveday sarcastically. 'Yes, there's only one copy. Roberta says her fingers would snap off at the knuckles if she had to type any more than that. So, we hire out the one we've got for sixpence a pop. All the girls at the school read it.'

Master Oliver Davenport smiled. 'And what do you do with the sixpences?'

'We buy gobstoppers, mostly,' said Loveday. 'We like gobstoppers.'

'But what if a girl doesn't *want* to hire the magazine for a shilling?' asked Horatio.

Loveday smiled serenely and sliced at the air with her lacrosse stick. 'I generally menace them until they do,' she said. 'It's supply and demand. I supply the magazine and then I demand money for it.'

'Isn't that extortion?' asked Horatio, perching on the arm of the chair.

'Quite possibly,' said Loveday, 'but it has kept me in gobstoppers this past term.'

Master Oliver Davenport walked to the window and leaned against the stone sill. Far below the boys' room, another taxi cab had drawn up outside the house.

'Who's she?' asked the boy as the driver opened the door and a large and elderly woman, dressed in green tweed, decanted herself on to the gravel drive. She wore thick grey stockings and stout shoes of brown patent leather.

'That's Great Aunt Henrietta,' said Horatio, joining Master Oliver Davenport at the window.

'She's a writer.'

'A real writer? You mean books and things?'

'Oh yes,' said Horatio. 'The sort where somebody gets bumped off and everybody has a motive. Then in the final chapter it usually turns out that it was the butler who carried out the dark deed.'

'She's awfully famous,' said Loveday. 'She even has her own waxwork at Madame Tussauds.'

'I never understand the way people behave in murder mystery books,' pondered Master Oliver Davenport, crunching down on a nugget of peanut brittle. 'You know, the way everybody carries on having lunch and supper and things as though they've quite forgotten that somebody's been done in and there's a murderer in their midst. I think a grisly killing or two might put me off my food.'

'It doesn't seem to worry the Great Aunt,' said Horatio. 'And she's solved countless murders.'

Master Oliver Davenport's eyes opened wide in horror. 'Real murders?' he asked.

Loveday nodded. 'Oh absolutely,' she said.

'Scotland Yard have her portrait on a wall somewhere.'

'I'd like to solve crimes when I grow up,' said Eustace, who had been giving the matter consideration for much of his young life. 'It would be ripping stuff to have a nice jolly murder to sink my teeth into.'

'What about us?' said Loveday. 'You don't think we're going to leave you to solve crimes all on your own, do you?'

Eustace smiled. 'I always imagined you'd be more likely to commit crimes than solve them,' he said.

'I did think about becoming a mercenary or something,' said Loveday, grasping her lacrosse stick with both hands and swinging it like a broadsword. 'I quite liked the idea of skirmishes in far-off lands.'

Just then Master Oliver Davenport's stomach rumbled mournfully.

'Sounds like it's high time we went in search of cake,' said Horatio, heading for the door. 'Come on.' He stopped suddenly and turned, his arms raised in front of him and his voice dropping to a bass rumble. 'But keep an eye out for Old Bramble Head. We're not the only ones with an appetite on Michaelmas Eve!'

Chapter Three

And What of Watkins?

THE CHILDREN RAN down the stairs from the attic rooms, back along the landing of family portraits and down the great oak staircase to the hall. Percival was busily carrying Great Aunt Henrietta's suitcases inside out of the rain. The Great Aunt herself had pulled a walking cane from the elephant's-foot umbrella stand and was evidently considering its suitability as a violent weapon. 'Put your back into it, man,' she commanded, tapping the cane sharply against the wooden floor. 'I have a book to write. This is no time to dawdle!'

'Quickly,' whispered Horatio. 'Before she sees us and enlists our help to haul her cases upstairs.'

'Through here,' said Eustace, pushing open a hidden door behind the stuffed bear.

'Does this take us to the dungeons?' asked Master Oliver Davenport, as he followed the children down a steep flight of stone steps that seemed to lead to the very depths of the manor house.

'Something like that!' shouted back Horatio, as he thundered down the stairs. 'How do you fancy being stretched on the rack? We can have you an inch or two taller by dinnertime.'

Master Oliver Davenport swallowed hard.

'Oh my giddy aunt,' cried a woman's voice from below. 'Like a great herd of cattle running down them stairs!'

Reaching the bottom of the staircase and rounding a corner, the children arrived in the kitchen of Bleakley Manor. They passed an enormous oak dresser that stretched from the flagstone floor to the vaulted ceiling, topped by a row of gleaming copper jelly moulds that sparkled in the glare of electric light.

Ahead of them, by the long kitchen table, stood

Cook. She was a short woman with a round, pink face and greying hair pulled back beneath a white cap. She beamed as the children approached. 'I thought it was marauding pirates, from the sound of you,' she laughed.

'You said it sounded like a herd of cattle,' protested Horatio.

'Cows or pirates,' said Cook, with a shrug. 'One or t'other.' She wiped her red hands on her apron and put on her spectacles. 'Well, haven't you grown since last Michaelmas, Master Eustace! And Miss Loveday, pretty as a partridge. The very spit of your mother, you are.'

'And this is Master Oliver Davenport,' said Eustace.

Cook smiled. 'Right good it is to meet you,' she said, taking the boy's outstretched hand and shaking it warmly.

'Is that jam roly-poly pudding for dinner tonight?' asked Horatio, as Cook floured the table and rolled out a crust of suet pastry.

'It most certainly is,' said Cook. 'Didn't think I'd let you go hungry on your first day back from school, did you?'

'You're an absolute sport,' said Horatio admiringly. 'One of the right sort and no mistake.'

'Need to feed you up a bit, I reckon, Master Horatio,' said Cook, blushing from the compliment and spreading the pastry thickly with raspberry jam. 'Looks like they're half-starving you at that school of yours. The clothes are near hanging off you.'

'The thing is,' replied Horatio, sombre-faced, 'they don't like us to get too fat. They think it makes our brains sluggish. We get hardly more than three square meals of gruel a day. And a buttered turnip for high days and holidays.'

Cook looked alarmed.

'He doesn't mean it,' said Eustace, pummelling Horatio on the arm.

Loveday grinned at Master Oliver Davenport. 'And besides,' she said, 'if they did starve them to death there'd be complaints from the parents.'

'That's to say, *some* of the parents,' added Horatio, rubbing his arm. 'Not our parents, obviously.'

'Oh, Master Horatio,' said Cook, with a gurgling laugh. 'The wicked awful things that come out of that head of yours! Don't you listen to a word of it, Master Oliver. Not a word!'

But Master Oliver Davenport did not reply; he was staring absently into space. 'Buttered turnips,' he murmured hungrily. 'They must be delicious.'

With a respectful cough to announce his arrival, Horton appeared from the kitchen staircase.

'Have a drop of tea, will you, Mr Horton?' asked Cook, lifting up the pot and swilling round the tea leaves.

'Thank you, but no,' replied Horton stiffly. 'I merely wished to inform you that there will be ten for dinner tonight.' He smiled at the children, though Eustace felt certain that the man was displeased to see them sprawled out around the kitchen table. With a slight nod of his head, Horton turned and headed for the butler's pantry at the far end of the kitchen, pulling the door shut behind him.

The children were given ginger cake and cold milk and they watched as Cook tied up the suet pudding and dropped it into a large pan of bubbling water.

'What happened to Watkins?' asked Horatio as Cook sat down with a cup of hot, sweet tea and waited for the pudding to boil. 'It was a dashed surprise to see him gone and the new chap in his place.'

'Now there's a tale,' said Cook lowering her voice. 'Took sick, Mr Watkins was.' She shook her head. 'At least that's what they *said*.'

'What who said?' asked Eustace excitedly. He pulled out his pocket notebook and pencil, sensing a mystery in the offing.

'Tell on,' said Horatio eagerly, helping himself to another slice of ginger cake.

'Well, that's what's so strange,' said Cook, taking the children into her confidence. 'Mr Watkins was fond of a tipple. Every night he'd cross the bridge into the village for a glass of rum and shrub at the

Stoat and Raven. As regular as clockwork.' She frowned and waved a stubby finger at the children. 'Course, I don't touch a drop myself. Except what's medicinal and improving for the constitution. My mother warned me of the evils of drink.' She stopped. 'Where was I? Oh, yes. Well, one night, as soon as the Master had gone up to bed, Mr Watkins set out for the Stoat and Raven as usual. Only he never came back. I was worried he'd fallen off the bridge and drowned himself in the marsh. I didn't want to concern the Mistress, so I waited down here in case the telephone should ring with awful terrible news.'

'And did it ring?' asked Loveday.

Cook nodded. 'That it did, miss. The telephone in Mr Watkins' pantry, it was. Near frightened the life out of me. It was gone eleven, by the kitchen clock.'

Master Oliver Davenport leaned forward expectantly. 'And had something awful terrible happened to the man?' he asked.

'No, Master Oliver, not as such,' said Cook, taking a deep slurp of her tea. 'I didn't recognise the gentleman's voice on the other end of the line, but he told me he was a friend from the pub. Not that Mr Watkins was in the habit of fraternising with the villagers, mind you, and that's what was so peculiar about it. Said Mr Watkins had knocked back his glass of rum and shrub and then come over all peculiar.'

'In what way peculiar?' asked Master Oliver Davenport, helping himself to a second and third slice of ginger cake. 'Drunk as a lord, you mean?'

'I don't mean that at all,' said Cook, frowning reproachfully at the boy and returning the ginger cake to its tin. 'I've never known Mr Watkins to drink more than was right and proper for a man in his position. Peculiar sick, I means. Always been a martyr to gallstones, Mr Watkins. Played him up something rotten.'

'And what happened next?' asked Loveday, impatient to reach the conclusion of the story and hopeful that it would involve revolvers or cutlasses.

'Then Mr Horton arrived by taxi cab the very

next morning, in time to carry the mistress up her breakfast tray,' continued Cook, taking another sip of tea.

'But didn't you think it was all rather odd?' asked Eustace, curious that Cook had not been more thorough in her investigations. 'One butler disappearing and another butler arriving out of the blue like that?'

'It's a fool who questions every odd thing that happens in this place,' answered Cook, draining the dregs from her teacup. 'Odd things going on here morning, noon and night, if you asks me. Which you didn't. But there, it's off my chest.' She opened a drawer in the kitchen table and pulled out a picture postcard. 'I had this from Mr Watkins just the other day. Have a read of it, if you like.'

Horatio took the postcard. On the front was a gaudy picture of yellow sands and two donkeys, with the words 'Wish You Were Here'. He turned over the card and slowly deciphered the spidery handwriting:

*Wishing as how you was here, Cookie.
On the mend now, though I was
terrible sick. Don't worry yourself
on my account as I've retired to a
boarding house with sea views and
developed a taste for the excellent
pickled winkles they serve hereabouts.
Best compliments and hope as this
finds you well.*

Watkins

'Is there a postmark?' asked Loveday.

'Yes, look,' said Horatio, holding out the card. 'Merrywolde-on-Cliffe.'

'That postcard put my mind at rest, I don't mind telling you,' said Cook. 'What if Mr Watkins had been done to death, I'd been thinking, and chopped up into tiny little pieces? Like the awful terrible things you read about in the newspapers. That would never do.'

Eustace cast an eye towards the butler's pantry. 'And what's Horton like?' he asked.

'Keeps himself to himself,' said Cook. She lowered her voice and leant forward in her chair. 'I'll tell you this much though; he's got airs and graces. I've said it before and I'll say it a thousand times, there are some butlers what think they're a cut above their masters, and it never ends well.' She hauled herself out of the chair and straightened her apron. 'Now, you run along or there won't be a thing to eat for dinner, and then you'll be grumbling at me.'

'How strange,' said Master Oliver Davenport as the children climbed the staircase from the kitchen, 'that your aunt didn't write to tell you that the butler had been taken ill. If he was a special chum of yours.'

'Aunt Maude isn't frightfully good at spotting things like disappearing butlers,' said Horatio with a grin.

Loveday laughed. 'I doubt she even noticed that Horton wasn't Watkins!'

'Master Oliver Davenport is right though,' said Eustace, who had been troubled by Cook's story.

'There is something decidedly murky about this business. And if Aunt Maude isn't going to ask questions, then we jolly well should!'

Eustace, Horatio, Loveday and Master Oliver Davenport continued on upstairs, passing Violet, the parlourmaid, as she scurried by with fresh linen. She was a tall young woman with dark hair and a pale, sad face.

'Hello, Violet,' said Loveday. 'It's good to see you haven't abandoned the sinking ship as well.'

'Where else would I go, miss?' answered Violet. 'I'll be here till I drops down dead or they carts me off to the loony bin … whichever comes soonest.' She gave an uncertain smile and hurried downstairs.

The children were startled by the loud blast of an approaching motor horn. Running to the nearest window and opening it wide, they were in time to see a sleek, green open-topped sports car as it tore up outside the house. With a violent screech of brakes the car skidded to a halt, sending a shower of gravel high into the air.

'What-ho, Uncle Rufus!' called down Horatio.

The driver grinned as he removed his motoring goggles. 'What-ho, nephews and niece!' he cried. 'What-ho, one and all!' With another blast of the motor horn he continued along the drive to the garages at the back of the house.

'That's our Uncle Rufus. He's an awful cad!' said Cousin Loveday adoringly.

'I say,' said Master Oliver timidly, 'do you think your other uncle might be here yet? You know, Colonel Theodore Bleakley?'

'Why don't we go and see?' said Horatio. 'His room's just up here.'

The children hurried along the corridor, Horatio leading the way.

'Is this the place?' asked Master Oliver Davenport in a reverent whisper as Horatio stopped outside a closed door.

'That's right,' said Horatio. 'Well, knock then,' he said to Master Oliver Davenport. '*You're* the hero-worshipper.'

Master Oliver Davenport's face flushed a bright shade of mauve.

'Don't be an ass, Horatio,' said Eustace, and rapped three times at the door.

There was no reply.

Eustace turned the handle and entered the room. It smelled strongly of stale tobacco smoke and was stacked from floor to ceiling with ancient artefacts. There were Roman oil lamps, stone busts of Greek warriors, fragments of mosaic, Egyptian jackal-headed canopic jars, and pots of every shape and size. The large desk in the centre of the room was almost entirely hidden beneath battered filing boxes and old archaeological maps, and a large terracotta bust sat in front of the fireplace, wrapped up carefully in a grey blanket.

A loud snore issued from the corner of the room.

Loveday giggled and nudged Master Oliver Davenport, pointing to a canvas tent that had been strung from an enormous mahogany bookcase, stretching across to a stack of wooden packing cases that were piled beside the desk. Another loud snore came from within.

Eustace coughed politely. There was an explosive snort and Colonel Theodore appeared on hands and knees from behind a mosquito net. He was a pleasant-faced man, wearing a baggy and moth-eaten pullover. His sandy-coloured hair was long and curly and his skin was chestnut brown from years spent excavating far-flung burial sites. 'Must have nodded off,' he laughed, climbing to his feet and brushing himself down. 'I see I'm overrun by an enemy tribe of nephews and nieces and … ?'

'Master Oliver Davenport,' said Master Oliver Davenport.

The Colonel slipped a small vase of mottled green glass from his pocket and held it up to the visitors. 'Know what this is, eh? Bet you half a crown you don't.'

'It's a tear flask,' replied Master Oliver Davenport, who had recently read an article on the very subject. 'They were used by mourners at funerals of the ancients.'

'Very good, very good,' said the Colonel with an

approving nod of his head. 'A most intelligent boy.'

'Do I get my half-crown now, sir?' asked Master Oliver Davenport.

The Colonel's hearing seemed suddenly to fail him and he turned quickly from the boy and began rooting around in one of the packing cases. 'Ah-ha!' he exclaimed. 'Now this artefact might interest you. A carved scarab beetle from Egypt … from the Twelfth Dynasty, in point of fact.' He carefully removed the object, which had been wrapped tightly in a sheet of newspaper. 'Dug it up myself at a most interesting site, a day's journey from Cairo.' But before he could unwrap the carving, Horatio gasped and pointed desperately at his uncle's sleeve. A small orange scorpion had scuttled from the folds of newspaper and was making its way quickly along the Colonel's right arm.

'A scorpion, Uncle!' cried Eustace.

Without a moment's hesitation, the Colonel shook his arm sharply, flicking the scorpion from his sleeve and sending it somersaulting towards the desk. The creature landed on its back and struggled to right itself, kicking its legs wildly in the air.

Master Oliver Davenport gave an anguished howl and stepped away from the desk, tripping over another packing case and falling backwards into Colonel Theodore's tent.

Loveday snatched up an empty drinking glass and crept stealthily towards the desk. The scorpion scuttled round to face the girl, its tail arched and its stinger trembling, but Loveday was too quick – she pounced and trapped the creature neatly beneath the upturned glass. 'Got it!'

'That was a thrilling development,' said Eustace weakly, his heart racing in his chest.

'Now, let's have a good look at you, my fine friend,' said Colonel Theodore, slipping a sheet of paper beneath the glass and holding it up to the electric light so that he could examine the creature more closely. 'A remarkable specimen. Quite incredible, the wildlife I seem to have brought home with me from Egypt.'

'You mean you've seen other exotic creatures

here, Uncle?' asked Horatio, helping Master Oliver Davenport to his feet and disentangling the boy from the swathes of mosquito netting.

'Oh yes,' said the Colonel. 'Just this morning I found a snake in my bed. Your Aunt Maude nearly had some manner of fit.' He dropped the scorpion into an empty cardboard box and closed the lid. 'I'll deal with you later,' he murmured, with an ominous smile.

'What is this, sir?' asked Master Oliver Davenport, pointing to a small round object, forged from ancient copper, which hung from a hook on the wall.

'Was it used for murdering people from the past?' suggested Loveday. 'I do hope so.'

'No, no,' said the Colonel, his eyes sparkling with delight as he reached up to retrieve the artefact from its hook. 'This is a Grecian nose harp. I have become an authority on the instrument and perhaps the only man living who can recreate the glorious music of the ancients.' He held the nose harp to his right nostril and blew hard. It was a peculiar noise, like the cry of a strangulated cat, but less enjoyable. Though it was not a tuneful instrument, it was clear to the children that it had worked its own peculiar brand of musical magic on the Colonel and he closed his eyes and smiled in ecstasy. The children, however, did not fall under the nose harp's mystic spell, so when they heard the dressing gong sounding loudly, they seized their opportunity to slip from the room and return to the nursery wing to dress for dinner.

'The Colonel is what is referred to in polite society as an eccentric,' said Eustace as the boys readied themselves for the evening ahead, far from the mournful warbling of the nose harp.

'If that's what an eccentric is like,' said Master Oliver Davenport, as he struggled to do up his bow tie, 'then I'd jolly well like to be one as well one day.'

The door swung open violently and Loveday sloped into the room, wearing a dress of purple satin which was so long that she kept tripping over the hem. 'I look odd in dresses,' she complained.

'And it makes it much more difficult to climb trees and whatnot.'

'What's happened to your hair?' asked Eustace. 'You look as though you've been tied up like a parcel.'

'I did it with string,' said Loveday. 'Do you think anyone will notice? Only I used the ribbon Aunt Maude gave me to make a rat trap instead.'

'Great Aunt Henrietta will notice,' replied Horatio gloomily.

'She's certain to,' agreed Eustace. 'The Great Aunt never misses a thing.'

'If I were in your place I'd be thankful to have any living relative at all,' said Master Oliver Davenport. 'She can't really be as bad as all that.'

'I'll let that pass because you haven't met her yet,' said Horatio, as a second gong sounded from the distant dining room.

'Five minutes until grub's up!' grinned Loveday, hitching up the hem of her dress. 'Race you downstairs!'

The children ran from the room. Master Oliver

Davenport, who it seemed could show remarkable bursts of speed whenever food was in the offing, led the way downstairs.

Chapter Four

As Midnight Approaches

THE CHILDREN ENTERED the dining room and Master Oliver Davenport marvelled at the sight before him. It was a cavernous place, with high panelled walls and a long row of deer antlers mounted on mahogany shields. Everywhere around him was polished wood and gleaming silver.

Sir Max Bleakley sat at the far end of the long dining table. He had side-whiskers and a walrus moustache, and wiry grey hairs had erupted at each earhole. Whether the evening suit he wore was too small or Sir Max was too large was a matter for debate. But Ludd-on-Lye was a remote village where tailors seldom set foot.

Aunt Maude, dressed in a long violet evening gown and black pearls, sat at the opposite end of the table to Sir Max. Mustard and Pickle lay at her feet, in the vain hope that an occasional morsel of food might fall their way.

Beside Sir Max sat Colonel Theodore, who did not own a dinner suit and had no intention of ever doing so. He was dressed instead in shorts and pullover and had not even brushed his hair. Across the table from the Colonel, wedged tightly into her seat, sat Great Aunt Henrietta, a monstrosity of tweed and pearls and saggy skin.

'Ah, good,' said Aunt Maude as a middle-aged man of the cloth timidly entered the room. 'This is the Reverend Edwin Saline-Crum.'

It was not unusual to the cousins to find Bleakley Manor playing host to odd and assorted members of the clergy. The doors of the house were often darkened by retired rectors or vacuous vergers who made a point of beating a pilgrimage to Ludd-on-Lye in aid of countless worthy causes. The specimen on display was hunched at the shoulders and his large eyes seemed to stick out like organ stops as he turned to face the children.

He smiled and sniffed and extended a lily-white hand. 'I'm delighted to meet you,' he said.

The Great Aunt held her spectacles to her eyes, inspecting the Reverend curiously. 'Your face is familiar to me,' she said. 'Do I know you?'

'I doubt it,' replied the Reverend with a nervous laugh. 'If you've seen one member of the clergy, you've seen us all.' He lowered his head and made his way quickly to the dining table.

What an odd fellow, thought Eustace, wishing he had his pocket notebook with him to record his observations.

'Come now, don't hover,' said Aunt Maude impatiently, and the children took their seats. 'Now where can Rufus be?'

'Late, as usual!' bellowed Sir Max.

A fierce gust of wind rattled the windows loudly.

Colonel Theodore smiled. 'On a night such as this

one can well believe that Old Bramble Head will rise from the marshes to claim another victim from the Bleakley family.' He lit his pipe, puffing so hard that he disappeared in a cloud of tobacco smoke. The Reverend Saline-Crum coughed and spluttered, fanning the smoke away with a sharp flick of his napkin.

'It's a myth and that's all it is,' growled Sir Max. 'You don't believe in the legend any more than I do. And besides, there hasn't been a death here at Michaelmas in years.'

'Can you really be certain though, Max?' continued the Colonel. 'Who's to say Old Bramble Head won't rise this very night, with his pockets full of blackberries, red and mauve … and his shoulders wreathed in brambles …'

Aunt Maude looked suddenly distracted and her hands shook.

'That's quite enough, Theodore,' snapped Great Aunt Henrietta.

Just then the door burst open and Aunt Maude

gasped. A figure stepped from the shadows and entered the room.

'What-ho, assembled Bleakleys and their guests,' beamed Uncle Rufus, free from motoring helmet and gauntlets now, and dressed for dinner. He was tall and slim, with a wolfish grin, a neatly clipped moustache and hair so dark and luxuriant that he might have stepped from the pages of *The Monthly Movie-Goer*. 'Hello, kids! So, what did you think of the new motor?' he asked. 'A thing of beauty, isn't she?'

'It's a Borgstein Twin-Speed,' said Horatio, who knew his cars.

'A Twin-Speed indeed,' said Uncle Rufus as he took a seat next to Aunt Maude. 'Trouble is, I pranged the bally thing on the way down here. Either I was going too quickly or the hedge accelerated.' He turned his attention to Master Oliver Davenport. 'And who are you, then?'

'This is Master Oliver Davenport,' offered Loveday before the boy had a chance to reply.

Uncle Rufus smiled and nodded. 'I heard my sister had taken pity on some poor waif and stray,' he said. 'I guess you must be the poor waif and stray of whom I speak?'

'I guess I must be,' said Master Oliver Davenport, summoning up his best and most practised waifish smile.

'I'm their diabolical Uncle Rufus,' said the uncle, running his fingers through his hair and grinning wickedly at the children. 'A pleasure to meet you.' He turned to Aunt Maude, who had been staring at him intently, and gave her a fond kiss on the cheek. 'Hello, Sis,' he said. 'Have you missed your beloved brother?'

Aunt Maude smiled and nodded. 'Oh, my dear Rufus,' she purred.

Eustace was always amazed to see the miraculous change that came over Aunt Maude whenever Uncle Rufus arrived. There was something different about her eyes – as though someone had flicked a switch and the light had finally come on.

Horton appeared with a silver tray of lamb cutlets and began to serve the family and guests. Percival entered and set a plate of steamed beetroot before Great Aunt Henrietta; it was a vegetable she consumed at every meal.

Uncle Rufus leaned towards Master Oliver Davenport. 'Seeing how ghastly the family is, I bet you're rather glad you're an orphan, aren't you?'

Thinking it impolite to agree or disagree, the boy said nothing.

'I'm only grateful that I'm not related to them by blood,' continued Uncle Rufus. 'If my sister hadn't married into the family, I'd give the lot of them a jolly wide berth. Have you read any of the Great Aunt's books? Frightful tripe. Each of them the size of a house brick but nowhere near as interesting.'

'Well?' said Sir Max, casting a brooding glance in the direction of the Reverend Saline-Crum. 'Going to say grace, are you?'

'Oh … I … well, if you think …' mumbled the Reverend, twisting his napkin nervously in his hands and looking for all the world like a man who wished the ground would open up and swallow him whole.

'You have to sing for your supper at Bleakley Manor,' growled Sir Max. 'My father used to keep a long stick for poking the clergy when they didn't behave. Used to prod 'em with it till they dashed well complied with his wishes. Now, I hope it won't come to that, eh, Reverend?'

The Reverend Saline-Crum mopped his glistening brow with the napkin and rose shakily from his chair. 'We give thanks for this splendid dinner laid out before us—'

'Good start,' interrupted Uncle Rufus. 'Now, give it some oomph, Rev!'

Eustace was watching Great Aunt Henrietta with curiosity. She was glaring more beadily than ever, and the full force of this glare was being directed at the Reverend Saline-Crum.

'We are not worthy of such bounty,' continued the Reverend. 'We are sinners to a fault.' He cast a furtive glance in the direction of the Great Aunt.

'But remember not the sinner for his *sin*. Look kindly upon his efforts to reform ... to put his wickedness behind him as he walks the path to righteousness. Amen.' He gave a weak smile, bowed his head and sat back down.

'Your soul might be heavy with sin, Reverend, but not mine,' snapped Sir Max. 'I asked for grace, not a whole blessed sermon.'

Uncle Rufus snorted with laughter and the Great Aunt silenced him with another of her frosty glares.

'Loveday, your hair!' exclaimed Aunt Maude, noticing for the first time that her niece's hair was tied up with knotted string. 'I thought I gave you a length of ribbon?'

'Oh yes,' said Loveday, slicing off a piece of her lamb cutlet and dipping it into a slick of mint sauce. 'You did. And jolly helpful it was too. I used it to make a rat trap.'

'I can't have heard you correctly, my dear,' interrupted Aunt Maude. 'I thought you said "rat trap".'

'That's right, Aunt Maude,' said Loveday. 'I'm hardly going to catch a rat *without* a trap, am I?'

To fill the uncomfortable lull in conversation, Colonel Theodore slipped the Grecian nose harp from his pocket and raised it to his left nostril.

But the Grecian nose harp was an acquired taste and it was instantly apparent that Great Aunt Henrietta had not acquired it. 'No,' she commanded, her voice booming across the table like a roll of thunder. 'I quite forbid you to play that thing at dinner.'

'But Aunt Henrietta—' protested the Colonel.

'No!' snapped the Great Aunt.

Miserably, Colonel Theodore dropped the nose harp back into his pocket.

'Are you keeping well, Great Aunt Henrietta?' asked Eustace politely, in a valiant attempt to keep the conversation going. 'I hear you're writing a new book.'

The Great Aunt peered over her spectacles at the boy. 'Of course I'm writing a new book,' she said.

'I'm a writer. It's what I do.'

'And will there be many dead bodies in it?' asked Loveday.

'Just enough,' replied the Great Aunt. 'That's what a good murder mystery needs. And a group of suspects who can't easily escape. It is to be called *A Medlar for the Bletting*.'

'Please, Madam,' said Master Oliver Davenport, who was not sure how best to address a person who had their own wax portrait at Madame Tussauds, 'what is bletting?'

The Great Aunt sighed irritably. 'It means to rot,' she said. 'A medlar is a type of fruit. It is a clever play on words which I do not expect you to understand.' She peered hard at the boy through her spectacles. 'I suppose *you* must be the Poor Unfortunate.'

'Yes,' replied Master Oliver Davenport.

'I have written Poor Unfortunates into my books,' said the Great Aunt. 'They always die.'

Master Oliver Davenport's jaw dropped.

Sir Max leaned forward in his chair, his eyes fixed

on the boy. 'New blood, eh?' he barked. 'Know anything about pickles, do you?'

'Very little, I'm afraid, sir,' replied Master Oliver Davenport.

'Ah,' said Sir Max gravely. 'Thought as much. That's the trouble with young people these days. Nobody knows the first thing about pickling. I was no older than you when I sold my first bottle of piccalilli.'

'Very interesting, sir,' lied Master Oliver Davenport.

'And do you know the chief ingredients of a bottle of Bleakley's Mustard Piccalilli?' Sir Max did not wait for an answer. 'Pure malt vinegar and—'

Aunt Maude looked up from her cutlet. 'There will be no more talk of pickling at the dinner table,' she said stiffly. 'You promised me faithfully that you would not experiment with a single relish, pickle or chutney the entire Michaelmas weekend …'

The words died on her lips as a sudden screaming gust of wind rattled the windows and the electric lights flickered. Colonel Theo of the opportunity to attempt a di conversation. 'I'm mounting another exp began.

'Over my dead body,' grunted Sir Max, wiping mint sauce from his moustache.

The Colonel looked wounded. 'But the treasures,' he protested, 'the buried riches that lie hidden, waiting to be discovered.'

'There are no great riches,' snapped Sir Max, banging the table hard with the handle of his knife to emphasise the point. 'There never are. And you're a fool if you think otherwise. All you ever bring back are pots. Pots of every shape and variety, I'll grant you, but still pots. Blasted pots!'

Aunt Maude attempted to pour oil on troubled waters. 'One or two of the pots are rather charming,' she ventured.

But Sir Max was not to be swayed. 'I'm forever forking out to fund his archaeological expeditions.'

'This one is different, Max,' insisted the Colonel,

most exciting

o more! It's like

l see you right, old

g the Colonel on the

ate man to snort a jet

dore took advantage
fferent topic of
dition,' he

'Of course,   t Aunt, cutting a thick slice of steaming beetroot. 'You would invest in any worthless cause, because you are profligate, Rufus.'

Horatio, who rarely read a book unless forced to, looked puzzled.

Eustace leaned across to whisper into his brother's ear. 'It means he wastes cash,' he explained.

'You would do well to live as I do, Rufus,' continued the Great Aunt. 'To leave your money in the bank and learn to exist on a diet that consists principally of beetroot and lemon barley water.'

It was clear to Eustace that it caused Sir Max physical discomfort and mental anguish to watch the

Great Aunt consuming beetroot in its naked state, and the man flinched as she took another mouthful.

'At least steamed beetroot makes a pleasant change from pickled beetroot,' said Uncle Rufus, under his breath.

'I won't hear you say a word against pickles,' said Sir Max, his moustache twitching as though it had suddenly taken on a life of its own. 'Not so long as you're under my roof.'

Uncle Rufus pushed his plate away. 'To be honest, Max, I don't have the faintest fascination with pickles or relishes. In fact, I'd go further … I'm not the slightest bit interested in preserved vegetables of *any* variety. I wish fervently that something bloody and awful would happen here, just so we had an interesting topic of discussion at the dinner table, and not blasted pickles at every bally gathering.'

'What on earth do you mean, Rufus?' exclaimed Aunt Maude.

'I'll tell you what I mean,' said Uncle Rufus, his eyes flashing mischievously. 'I pray that one dark and stormy night a ghastly murder might occur within these four walls.'

Eustace shot an anxious glance at Horatio, as a crack of thunder set the wolfhounds barking in alarm.

'You don't mean that, Rufus, dear. Of course you don't,' said Aunt Maude, tugging nervously at her pearls. 'You must curb this tendency towards the melodramatic, really you must.'

'Oh, but I *do* mean it, sister dearest,' said Uncle Rufus, warming to his theme. 'I mean it most sincerely. Something to alleviate the boredom ... assuming dear Old Bramble Head doesn't pay us a visit this Michaelmas. If person or persons unknown crept up the stairs to Max's room and coshed the old boy on the noggin ... well, just imagine how much livelier things would be around the hallowed halls of Bleakley Manor.'

'What's that you say?' gasped Sir Max, his eyebrows twitching.

'I think you'd look rather fetching with a dagger

in your back, old boy,' continued Uncle Rufus. 'Like an unfortunate victim in one of Aunt Henrietta's blasted books.'

'Not in front of the servants,' murmured Aunt Maude as Horton arrived, carrying in a *Bombe Neapolitan* on a large silver platter, and for a moment peace reigned supreme. The dessert was Cook's *pièce de résistance* – an enormous dome of sponge and ice cream, topped with piped swirls of meringue and studded with diamonds of emerald-green angelica. Percival followed behind at a respectful distance with the jam roly-poly pudding and a steaming jug of custard, which he carried towards the children.

Horatio cut himself a thick slice of the pudding. He passed Eustace the jug of custard and reached beneath the table to feed the wolfhounds a titbit of jam and suet pastry.

The servants departed and Uncle Rufus dug a silver serving spoon into the ice cream bombe, dolloping a mound of the dessert into his bowl. 'Of course,' he began again, his eyes darting slyly, 'I suppose that

I should come off rather well if anything *were* to happen to dear old Max.'

'And why the devil do you think that?' demanded Sir Max, glowering at Uncle Rufus from beneath beetling brows.

Aunt Maude lowered her eyes and refused to meet her brother's gaze.

'I wouldn't count on seeing a brass farthing from me,' continued Sir Max, slurping a spoonful of ice cream.

Uncle Rufus dropped his spoon. 'And why not?'

'Because I might very well decide to change my will, that's why not,' barked Sir Max, reddening from the collar up. 'I might not leave a penny to any of you … not to you, Theodore. Not even to you, Maude. And *then* where will you be, Rufus, without your sister to bail you out? Penniless, that's where!'

Eustace watched Aunt Maude closely as she scowled at her husband and stabbed slowly and repeatedly at a slice of meringue with the prongs of her fork.

Sir Max was clearly enjoying the spectacle of his family's discomfort. 'In fact,' he said, in conclusion, 'I might very well bequeath all my money to the orphans and widows of the pickling profession. And that'll be an end to your grasping once and for all!'

Horatio cut another slice of jam roly-poly pudding, and leaned towards his brother. 'It's just like Master Oliver Davenport said on the way here,' he whispered to Eustace, reaching over for the custard jug. 'The grasping relatives trying to get their hands on the old chap's loot. Now we just sit around and wait for the murder to occur!'

—◦—

'So, what do you think of the family so far?' Horatio asked Master Oliver Davenport as the boys prepared for bed. 'A priceless bunch, aren't they?'

The boy considered the question for some moments before answering. 'They are a rather unusual lot,' he replied, as delicately as possible.

'Quite,' said Eustace simply. He wound the alarm clock he had brought with him from school and placed it on his bedside table.

Master Oliver Davenport extracted a bag of pineapple cubes from his tuckbox and carefully laid a ring of the sweets on the floor around his bed.

'Whatever are you doing?' asked Horatio.

'It will distract the rats,' explained the boy. 'Better safe than sorry.'

Horatio seemed satisfied with this answer, and the pair settled down in their beds and fell promptly to sleep.

But sleep did not come so easily to Eustace. He tossed and turned for what seemed like hours before finally drifting off into a fitful sleep, only to be awakened by a howling wind and an eerie and persistent scrabbling at the window. His mouth was dry and his pulse raced as he glanced at the glowing green hands of his alarm clock – it was twelve midnight. He switched on his torch and pointed it at Horatio's bed.

'What is it?' groaned Horatio, blinking hard in the bright beam of light.

'I heard a noise,' whispered Eustace, glancing anxiously towards the window.

'It was Master Oliver Davenport, probably,' said Horatio. 'Listen to him. Snoring like a bunged-up hippo.'

'It wasn't snoring,' replied Eustace. 'It was something *else*.'

'Rats then,' said Horatio. 'Or perhaps Old Bramble Head himself!' He laughed, rolled over and went back to sleep.

Eustace settled down in bed, pointing his torch above him and following a large spider in the beam of light as it scurried across the ceiling and disappeared through a deep crack in the plaster. Pulling the blanket up over his head so he would not be seen by Old Bramble Head, he read from the pages of *The Big Book of Crime* by the light of the torch until he too fell asleep.

Chapter Five

A Murder at Michaelmas

IT WAS MICHAELMAS DAY and the storm had picked up. A howling wind whipped around the eaves of Bleakley Manor and the driving rain lashed against the window of the boys' bedroom. Spikes of lightning illuminated the sky, accompanied by the rolling roar of thunder.

Eustace stood, lost in thought, gazing out across the garden to the marsh beyond.

'Happy Michaelmas, one and all!' mumbled Horatio blearily, as Eustace's alarm clock rang out. 'You're up early.'

'I didn't sleep well,' said Eustace, switching off the alarm. 'I'm quite certain I heard something outside the window last night. It sounded distinctly like—'

'Not Old Bramble Head?' asked Master Oliver Davenport, rolling over in bed with a nervous laugh.

'You can count on it,' said Horatio, lowering his voice and reaching out to clutch Master Oliver Davenport tightly by the arm. 'Come to drag his next victim out to the marsh!'

As Master Oliver Davenport wriggled free from Horatio's clutches, there came a loud knock from outside.

'Who is it?' called Eustace anxiously.

'Happy Michaelmas, chaps!' grinned Loveday, flinging open the door. 'I've had a spot of luck. I didn't think it was going to work, but look!' Proudly, she reached into her pocket and pulled out a squirming grey rat. 'I'm going to train him,' she said. She set the rat down on the floorboards, with a piece of string tied round its waist as a harness, and watched delightedly as the creature munched upon the defensive ring of pineapple cubes around Master Oliver Davenport's bed. 'That's what I'll call him,' she laughed. 'Pineapple Cube!'

As soon as the children had safely imprisoned the rat in the chest of drawers, they made their way downstairs. Percival passed them in the hall, carrying a breakfast tray with a large silver teapot.

'That'll be for the Great Aunt,' Horatio explained to Master Oliver Davenport. 'She always has breakfast in bed. She says most of her characters come to her in dreams. She never stirs from her room until she's put pen to paper and captured it all.'

In the dining room, breakfast had been laid out in silver dishes on the sideboard. There were fried eggs and scrambled eggs, crisp rashers of bacon and a glistening mountain of sausages.

The wind howled down the chimney and the wolfhounds uttered an answering howl. Pickle's legs were trembling and Horatio gave the dog an encouraging pat on the head. 'This is the sort of day,' said the boy, 'when bad things happen. I think poor Pickle senses it. Old Bramble Head must have stirred from the marshes!' He cut into his fried egg, watching with satisfaction as the yolk bled out across the plate.

The clock on the mantelpiece chimed nine, and was echoed by the dull boom of the grandfather clock in the hall. As if running on clockwork herself, Aunt Maude arrived in the dining room. She appeared discouraged to find the children in attendance.

'Where is your uncle Max?' she inquired, glancing distractedly around the room. It was not the 'Happy Michaelmas' greeting the children were expecting, but Aunt Maude often defied expectations. 'It's most unlike him to be late for breakfast.' Sitting down at the table she poured herself a cup of coffee and buttered a slice of toast.

The clock was chiming the quarter hour when the door opened and Horton entered. He approached Aunt Maude's chair and bowed his head respectfully. 'There is an inspector at the door, madam,' he said.

Aunt Maude turned her head. 'An inspector?' she asked blankly. 'An inspector of *what*?'

Horton hesitated before speaking and lowered his

voice when he did. 'An Inspector of Police, madam,' he replied. 'He says he's come in regard to the corpse on the study floor.'

The children looked up in wide-eyed surprise and a slice of toast slipped from Horatio's fingers, to be snapped up by the wolfhounds.

'What did you say?' asked Eustace. 'A corpse?'

As Horton gave a gentle cough and repeated his message, a murmur of excitement passed between the children.

Aunt Maude rose from her chair with as much composure as she could muster.

Burning with curiosity, Eustace, Horatio and Loveday followed their aunt from the dining room. Master Oliver Davenport, who was conflicted by the prospect of leaving food uneaten, took a slice of toast and a sausage to fortify him on his way.

The front door stood open and the wind moaned around the echoing hall. A small man, no taller than Horatio, shivered on the threshold, umbrella in hand. He wore a black mackintosh coat, his collar raised to protect him from the driving rain.

'Is *this* the inspector?' asked Aunt Maude doubtfully.

The man cleared his throat and smoothed his moustache. 'Inspector Hanwell, madam,' he said. 'I've come about the body.'

'You must be mistaken,' replied Aunt Maude. 'There is no body.'

The Inspector left a measured pause, as if he was holding out hope that Aunt Maude had simply forgotten where she had left the body and would shortly provide him with the necessary information. As this information was not forthcoming, the Inspector spoke again. 'Look, madam,' he said. 'I'm not leaving here till I see a body.'

This was too much for Aunt Maude. 'I can't produce a corpse simply to oblige the police,' she protested. 'I can assure you, if there were a dead body tucked away somewhere in the house you would be the first to hear about it.'

Horton attempted to close the door but Inspector

Hanwell stopped it with his foot.

'Be that as it may, madam,' continued the Inspector slowly, 'I wouldn't feel that I'd carried out my right and proper duty if I didn't come in to investigate the matter further. I received a telephone call at Upper Bantree police station, informing me that if I was to come to Bleakley Manor at a quarter past the hour of nine I'd be sure to find a dead body on the floor of the study.'

'Very well then,' said Aunt Maude with a heavy sigh. 'I suppose you'd better come inside.'

Inspector Hanwell shook the rain from his umbrella and stepped into the hallway.

'How did you get here, Inspector?' asked Eustace, surprised not to see a police car parked outside the house.

'The police car at Upper Bantree had a flat tyre,' said the Inspector bitterly, as Horton took his umbrella and coat. 'I had to catch the train to Brockton Mannerley. There was no taxi cab to be had there, so I borrowed a bicycle from the stationmaster. I had to cycle all that way in the rain and thunder. The very least I expect for my troubles is a dead body.'

With Horton leading the way, the party continued along the hallway to Sir Max's study. The children waited with bated breath as the butler knocked at the door.

There was no answer.

'Max,' called Aunt Maude, 'will you open the door, please?'

Loveday reached out for the handle and attempted to turn it, but with no success.

'He never locks the door,' said Aunt Maude, an unmistakable note of anxiety creeping into her voice. 'Something must be wrong.'

Horton crouched down to peer through the keyhole.

'What can you see?' asked Aunt Maude impatiently.

Horton squinted hard. 'It's difficult to make out, madam.'

'Unlock the door, can't you?' said the Inspector. 'We need to get in and sort out this little mystery.'

But Horton shook his head. 'I'm afraid that can't be done, sir,' he said. 'The spare key from my pantry has been mislaid.'

Feeling round in his pocket, Horatio pulled out a paper clip and carefully unbent the wire. 'I know a little wheeze,' he said. 'Watkins taught it to me once, in case of dire emergency.' He inserted the wire into the lock and patiently moved it from side to side until a quiet but distinctive click could be heard. 'Now, Open Sesame!' he whispered, turning the handle and opening the door. He entered the room, followed by the children, Horton, the Inspector and Aunt Maude.

The curtains were closed and the study was in near darkness, though a lamp standing on the large desk in front of the window gave out a dull orange glow. It was a small, oak-panelled room with a low ceiling of black beams and ornate plasterwork, and the shelves were filled with clusters of old silver sporting trophies.

The body of a man lay sprawled on the floor beside

the fireplace. A stuffed crow, which had once taken pride of place in a case on the mantel, rested close to the man's head, surrounded by shards of broken glass. Around the figure's shoulders was a wreath of twisted brambles.

'Max!' gasped Aunt Maude, turning away in horror.

Eustace took a step towards the body. 'No, not him,' he whispered. 'It's the Colonel.' The man's features were contorted and his lips were stained purple from the blackberries that lay scattered about him.

Aunt Maude uttered a whimpering moan as the Inspector pushed Eustace aside and bent down over the body. 'And is he dead?' she murmured.

'Oh, he's dead all right,' said the Inspector. 'Dead as a doornail.'

Uncle Rufus appeared at the door and grinned at the assembled group. 'What's going on in here?' he asked. 'A little game of wink murder, is it?'

'It's too, too horrible,' groaned Aunt Maude,

growing suddenly ashen about the face. She toppled backwards in a dead faint, very nearly crushing the Inspector beneath her.

'Well, help me somebody!' cried the man, trying desperately to keep Aunt Maude upright.

Uncle Rufus sprang forward and helped to support his sister. 'Fetch the smelling salts, Horton!' he cried.

'Yes, sir,' replied Horton. 'I have them about my person, sir.' Horton removed a bottle from his waistcoat pocket, uncorked it and wafted it under Aunt Maude's nose. Her eyes flickered open and Uncle Rufus and Horatio helped her into an armchair.

'How are you feeling now, Sis?' asked Uncle Rufus.

'A little better, I think,' said Aunt Maude, and Horton re-corked the bottle.

'Whatever's all the noise?' came a voice and Sir Max strode purposefully into the room, evidently furious to see so many people gathered there. 'What the devil are you all doing in my study?'

Suddenly spotting the body laid out on the floor before him, he stopped.

'Theodore?' He leaned down and held a hand to the Colonel's cheek. 'His face,' he rasped. 'It's as cold as ice.' He shook his head. 'My poor, dear brother. My closest friend.'

Eustace raised an eyebrow. At dinner the night before it had seemed that all was not sweetness and light between his two uncles.

'We must telephone for the doctor,' said Uncle Rufus. 'I mean, oughtn't we?'

Aunt Maude stared hopelessly at the body. 'What will a doctor tell us that we don't already know for ourselves? The man's dead, isn't he?'

'He'd tell us *how* the Colonel died,' said Eustace. 'And if we know how he died, perhaps we can work out who dunnit.'

'Who *did* it,' corrected Aunt Maude. 'Murder is no excuse for poor grammar.'

'If I were you,' said Uncle Rufus, leaning towards the Inspector, 'I'd look no further than old Aunt Henrietta.

Her mind is a surging morass of murder and mayhem.'

Aunt Maude frowned. 'Do please be sensible, Rufus.'

'I am being sensible,' replied Uncle Rufus. 'She's forever turning us into characters in her blasted books. Maybe she went too far this time? Writers often come unstuck like that ... they can never quite tell the difference between fiction and real life.'

'What's that?' growled the Inspector. 'Who's he going on about?'

'My husband's aunt,' explained Aunt Maude. 'Henrietta Bleakley.'

The Inspector pursed his lips. 'That name's familiar to me,' he said. 'Now where've I heard it before ... ?'

'She is an author of popular crime novels,' interrupted Aunt Maude. 'And a close friend of the Commissioner of Scotland Yard.'

The Inspector frowned. 'That's as good a place to start my investigations as any,' he said. 'In the meantime – no one leave this room. I'll be wanting to talk to each of you in turn. Now, if you'll show me the way to the lady's room.'

'We'll take you,' said Eustace.

The children led the Inspector into the west wing of Bleakley Manor and along a wide corridor, lined with suits of armour and glass cases full of silver hunting trophies.

'Here we are,' said Eustace, stopping suddenly.

'This is the lair of the Great Aunt,' whispered Horatio, tapping gently at the door. 'All hope abandon, ye who enter here!' There was no answer so he knocked again, harder than before.

'Maybe she's been murdered as well?' was Master Oliver Davenport's gloomy assessment of the ensuing silence.

'Yes?' At last, Great Aunt Henrietta's barking voice could be heard from inside the room. 'What is it? Come in if you must.'

Horatio opened the door.

It was a dark and foreboding room, decorated with dull green wallpaper and heavy curtains of brown velvet. The Great Aunt sat at a tall oak bureau beside the window, tapping violently at a portable typewriter, her back turned to the door.

'Great Aunt Henrietta—' began Eustace, urgently.

'Don't talk,' commanded the Great Aunt. 'Don't utter a word, or I shall lose my thought.' Beside her typewriter stood a silver bowl, filled almost to overflowing with Devonshire clotted cream, which she consumed by the spoonful as she hammered away at the keys.

The visitors milled about silently as they waited for the Great Aunt to finish typing. It was an orderly room, and the tall bookcases that lined the walls were neatly stocked with every one of Great Aunt Henrietta's seventy-five murder mystery books. A small French clock took pride of place on the mantelpiece, with miniature golden daggers for hands. Beside the clock was a human skull, resting on a polished marble base with a brass plaque dedicated to the Great Aunt by the Society of Crime Authors.

Horatio was able to hold his tongue no longer and the words blurted out of him. 'We do have something frightfully urgent to talk to you about, Auntie.'

Great Aunt Henrietta turned slowly in her chair, holding her spectacles to her eyes and glowering fiercely at Horatio. 'If you call me *Auntie* again I'll write you as a character in my next book and I'll make quite certain that you die a slow and painful death.' Inspector Hanwell was lurking impatiently in a corner and the Great Aunt squinted in his direction. 'Who is this? Another young friend?'

The Inspector grimaced and was opening his mouth to protest when the Great Aunt raised her hand and stopped him in his tracks. 'I shall give you sixpence each if you promise never to disturb me at my work again.'

The Great Aunt's terms seemed agreeable and so the children lined up to receive their sixpences in turn.

The Inspector was now slowly grinding his teeth together. 'The reason I'm here, madam—'

'Quickly! Don't dawdle, I have work to do,' interrupted the Great Aunt, dipping a hand into her purse and retrieving a final sixpence which she held out to the man. Inspector Hanwell took the coin and dropped it into his waistcoat pocket. 'Now what do you say?'

'Thank you,' growled the Inspector.

'And what is it that you have come dressed as?' inquired the Great Aunt, looking the man up and down and evidently disapproving of her findings.

The Inspector's face flushed an unhealthy shade of purple. 'I'm dressed as a police inspector,' he rasped.

'And why is that?' demanded the Great Aunt.

'Because, madam,' replied the Inspector with quiet dignity, 'I am a Police Inspector.'

The Great Aunt uttered an unpleasant snort of a laugh. 'One knows one is getting older when the police start getting smaller.'

'Now look here,' began the Inspector, 'there's no need to be getting all personal.'

The Great Aunt returned to her typing. 'And why have you come to Bleakley Manor?' she barked, above the crashing of the keys.

'He's here because of the dead body,' shouted Loveday.

There was a pause and the typewriter fell silent.

'Dead body?' bellowed Great Aunt Henrietta, swinging round in her chair like a bloodhound catching the scent of something meaty. She rose up and towered above Inspector Hanwell, who gave a nervous, spluttering cough and took a step backwards. 'Well?' she demanded. 'What dead body? Speak, man!'

'I ... I ... well, I received a telephone call,' stuttered the Inspector. 'I was informed that if I was to come to Bleakley Manor this morning at a quarter past nine then I'd find a dead body laid out on the study floor.'

'And was the body in the study?' inquired the Great Aunt.

'Yes,' said Horatio. 'It was Colonel Theodore.'

'Then I must look into this mystery at once,' said the Great Aunt, rising from her chair and striding from the room with the Inspector and children in tow.

'Do you have any ideas, Aunt Henrietta?' asked Sir Max, as the woman surveyed the study with a steely gaze.

'It's quite evident how the Colonel was killed,' said the Great Aunt. 'He has been struck on the back of the head with the stuffed crow.'

Loveday reached down and scooped up a handful of the fallen blackberries.

'Liked blackberries, did he?' asked the Inspector.

'Do you think it was Old Bramble Head?' asked Master Oliver Davenport, his eyes wide as saucers.

'Superstitious nonsense,' snapped the Great Aunt. 'I do not believe that such a thing as a supernatural being exists.'

The Inspector rocked backwards and forwards, his boots creaking unpleasantly. 'I don't believe in ghosts and ghouls and mumbo-jumbo either,' he said firmly. After examining the windows carefully, the Inspector turned his attention to the desk. He opened each drawer in turn, carefully sifting through the contents.

'What's this, I wonder?' said Uncle Rufus, reaching beneath the desk and retrieving a long, folded document.

'I'll have that, thank you, sir,' said the Inspector, snatching the document away from the man. 'Last Will and Testament, eh? Interesting. Very interesting.'

'I'd threatened to change my will,' explained Sir Max sourly, tugging the paper from the Inspector's hands. 'Everyone's always grasping for my money.'

'And did you change your will, sir?' asked the Inspector.

'I did,' said Sir Max. 'I telephoned to my solicitor on the mainland. He arranged to drive over next week to make everything legal and binding.'

Uncle Rufus was slowly edging around the room towards the open door. 'Well, this has been quite the little tragedy,' he said. 'I'll miss the old chap. But I've got to scoot now, I'm afraid.'

The Inspector took a step backwards and pushed the door shut. 'I'm afraid I can't let you do that, sir.'

Uncle Rufus glared at the man. 'And why the devil not?' he demanded.

'I'm not letting anybody go until I'm satisfied of their innocence,' said the Inspector. 'Or to put it another way, until I'm sure they're not guilty.'

'Now wait just one minute,' protested Uncle Rufus, 'I don't know what it is you think you're accusing me of.'

'I'm not accusing of you of anything ... yet,' said the Inspector, a sly smile twitching about his lips.

Uncle Rufus stared hard at the man. 'Are you kneeling down?' he asked. 'Or is that your actual height?'

Inspector Hanwell glared back at Uncle Rufus and attempted to push himself up on tiptoe. 'I don't like your sort much,' he said.

'And what sort's that?' replied Uncle Rufus.

'The snooty sort,' said the Inspector.

'How do we know you're *really* an inspector

anyway?' asked Uncle Rufus, his eyes narrowing. 'Rather suspicious, I call it, turning up here out of the blue like this, the very moment that one of the family's been done in.'

'But I *am* an inspector,' insisted the Inspector.

'That's who you *claim* to be, certainly,' said Uncle Rufus. 'But then, of course, a murderer might very well say that.'

'A wolf in inspector's clothing, as it were,' said Eustace, and the Inspector scowled at the boy.

Uncle Rufus nodded. 'That may not even be a real moustache he's wearing,' he continued. 'Looks dashed suspicious to me.' He reached out and tugged hard at Inspector Hanwell's moustache.

'The moustache is attached, thank you, sir,' said the Inspector, wincing in pain. He took out his warrant card and held it close to Uncle Rufus's face, or as close as his short arms would allow.

Uncle Rufus read the warrant card with some disappointment. 'I suppose his story adds up,' he said, as the Inspector snatched the card away and returned it to his pocket. 'But it pays to be cautious.'

'Well, *somebody* must be responsible for the murder,' grunted Sir Max. 'My unfortunate brother certainly didn't clobber *himself* with the crow, did he?'

Eustace picked up the receiver from the telephone on Sir Max's desk and held it to his ear. 'Operator?' he whispered urgently. '*Operator?*' But answer came there none; the line was dead.

'What is it, Eustace?' asked Aunt Maude, her voice little more than a whisper. 'Whatever is the matter?'

'I think the line is down,' said Eustace, slowly replacing the receiver.

'Or else it's been cut,' said Uncle Rufus with a dark twinkle in his eye. 'Old Bramble Head's work, I'll be bound. I expect he's preparing to pick off the Bleakleys one by one!'

Outside, the winds raged and Aunt Maude moaned once more as the electric lights flickered.

Suddenly, Percival burst into the room, his clothes drenched by the rain. 'The bridge,' he panted. 'It's been struck by lightning. The legs have given way and it's all come crashing down into the marsh!'

'Then we're completely cut off from the mainland,' said Master Oliver Davenport, the colour draining from his face. 'And we're all alone on the island with a murderer!'

'There must be a boat moored up outside,' said Inspector Hanwell with a snort. 'There's a body wants collecting. It's not the correct way of things to leave corpses lying around gathering dust.'

'We didn't need a boat before,' said Eustace. 'We had a bridge.'

'And don't raise your hopes that the inhabitants of Ludd-on-Lye will rush out to our aid,' barked Sir Max. 'The village is two miles away and the people are too superstitious to venture in this direction at Michaelmas.'

Great Aunt Henrietta turned accusingly to the Inspector. 'Who was it that suggested you should visit Bleakley Manor today?' she demanded.

'I ... I ... well, I received a telephone call,' stammered the Inspector.

'And was the voice that of a man or a woman?' persisted the Great Aunt.

'It was a muffled sort of a voice,' said the Inspector, shifting uneasily on the spot. 'Indistinct, if you take my meaning.'

Mustard was scratching at a wooden panel beside the fireplace and the Inspector turned angrily.

'Get that filthy great mutt out of here,' he barked. 'Interfering and a-tampering with vital police evidence.' He ushered the dog, and the family, towards the door. 'I need chalk to draw round the body,' he said, prodding Horton in the chest. 'And be quick about it.' Horton bristled, but nodded his head and hurried away. 'The rest of you can kindly leave me to my investigations,' concluded the Inspector with a self-satisfied smirk

Great Aunt Henrietta, who was not one to be hurried, turned beetroot-purple and the children prepared for fireworks.

'Investigations, indeed!' bellowed the Great Aunt. 'I shall solve this case as I have solved countless other mysteries. And if you get in my way, Inspector, then you will have the Commissioner of Scotland Yard to answer to!'

Inspector Hanwell gulped as Great Aunt Henrietta turned on her heel and stalked from the room.

Chapter Six

Too Many Sleuths

EUSTACE WAS TROUBLED. He had been waiting his entire life for a murder to occur and, now that it had, he was not sure how best to proceed. Of one thing he was certain: where there was a dead body there would be suspects and motives and a golden opportunity to outsmart Great Aunt Henrietta and an Inspector of Police.

'Do you have any theories?' Horatio asked, as Inspector Hanwell pushed at the stuffed crow with the toe of his boot.

'Some unhinged maniac, I shouldn't wonder,' said the Inspector. 'Some escaped prisoner, perhaps. Or a madman from a lunatic asylum.'

Eustace clicked his tongue as he pondered matters.

He bent down and scraped up a scattering of rust-brown dust that lay about the floor by the Colonel's shoulders. 'If it *was* a madman, then presumably he came in through the front door,' he said. The Inspector stared quizzically at the boy. 'Well, you examined the windows. They were all locked from the inside, were they not?' Eustace had quickly discovered that whenever he ended a sentence with the words 'were they not', 'was it not' or 'did it not' it had the desired effect of rattling the Inspector.

'I bet you don't even have a fingerprint kit, let alone any theories!' said Loveday.

'Ha!' smirked the Inspector, taking a tin from his pocket and opening it up to reveal a brush and dusting powder. 'You've lost that bet then, haven't you?' He turned his back on the children and set to work.

Loveday attempted to peer over the Inspector's shoulder as he dusted for fingerprints. 'I don't expect you'll find anything useful,' she said. 'No murderer worth his salt would be stupid enough to leave prints.'

'That's where you and me we've got a fundamental difference of opinion,' said the Inspector.

Eustace shook his head. 'You and *I*,' he corrected.

'Don't you get clever with me,' sniped the Inspector. 'I know my grammar, thank you very much. I knew my times tables at eight and I won the class prize for poetry recitation before I even made it to my twelfth birthday. What do you think of that?'

'I didn't have you down as the poetic type,' said Eustace.

'I wandered lonely as a thingummy,' said the Inspector, 'so there. Now don't you go touching things and snooping round,' he warned them. 'There'll be valuable clues and the like. Don't want you brats upsetting the handcart.'

'I never thought I'd see an *actual* corpse,' said Loveday, staring at the prostrate body of the Colonel with undisguised fascination. 'But now here one is, stretched out in front of me, as large as life.'

'An unfortunate turn of phrase,' said Eustace.

'You're ghoulish,' said the Inspector, 'that's what you are.'

'Can we help you draw lines around the body?' asked Loveday when Horton returned with the chalk.

'No, you can't,' said the Inspector. 'It's not right and it's not decent having children drawing lines around corpses. And quite apart from that, it's against police procedure.'

He carefully drew a chalk line around the body. It was evidently one of his favourite pastimes and he whistled as he worked.

'*Is* there any police procedure?' asked Eustace, his eyebrows arching ironically. 'I thought you were just making it up as you went along.'

Inspector Hanwell bristled. 'That's enough of your cheek. Now, clear off, the lot of you, and leave me to my investigations!'

'The poor old Colonel,' said Horatio, following Eustace from the study and out into the hallway. 'To be murdered by mistake like that … instead of Uncle Max.'

Eustace frowned. 'But what if Uncle Max never was the intended victim?'

Loveday gazed at her cousin with wide eyes. 'You think the murderer intended to bump off Colonel Theodore all along?'

'I don't know,' said Eustace. 'But he was almost stung by the scorpion … and he told us that he found a snake as well. I think that gives us reason to suspect that matters are not quite as they appear.'

'Why anybody would go to the trouble of killing him, I really don't know,' said Horatio. 'Fate is normally pretty effective at despatching members of the Bleakley family. If a tree falls over or a bolt of lightning strikes, chances are you'll find a Bleakley standing in the self-same spot. It would seem quite unnecessary for mortal man to take matters into his own hands.'

'Or *her* hands,' added Eustace.

Loveday lowered her voice to a respectful whisper. 'Never more will Colonel Theodore Bleakley warble on the nose harp.'

Master Oliver Davenport stared admiringly at Loveday. 'That's almost poetry,' he said.

Loveday flashed a smile at the boy. 'It's how I'll start my article for *Murder and Mayhem Magazine*,' she said. 'Fruity stuff, isn't it? All we need to do now is find the culprit, and I won't even have to menace the girls at Miss Sunnybrook's for the next edition.'

Rounding a corner, the children very nearly collided with the Reverend Saline-Crum, who was standing at the bottom of the hall staircase, making a sketch of a stuffed squirrel in a glass case. He turned and nodded. 'My dear children,' he said, closing his sketchbook and nervously tapping his pencil against the cover. 'I have heard the shocking news about your unfortunate uncle.' He shook his head. 'Most, *most* shocking.' He tapped his sketchbook once more, his eyes darting anxiously between the four children. 'And I hear an Inspector of Police has arrived at the house? What of him?'

Eustace smiled to himself, feeling that the Reverend had finally alighted upon the topic of conversation that was uppermost in his mind. 'I expect he'll want to question each of us in turn,' he said. 'That's what detectives generally do … when someone is murdered.'

The Reverend gasped sharply, inhaling a small passing moth then coughing it back up. 'Quite so,' he spluttered. 'Quite so.'

The children continued along the hallway. Eustace stopped and called back over his shoulder. 'I hope you don't mind my asking, Reverend,' he said, 'but where were you at breakfast?'

The Reverend Saline-Crum, who was smearing the remains of the inhaled moth against his sketchbook, looked up at the boy in surprise. 'I … I was in my room,' he stammered. 'I am prone to bouts of nasal discomfort. The marsh waters that surround us on the island have unbalanced the cavities of my nose. After a menthol inhalation, I returned to my bed. It was ten o'clock before I woke again.'

'I'm very sorry to hear of your nasal discomfort,' said Eustace crisply, watching with curiosity as the

Reverend bowed his head and skulked away towards the drawing room.

'There's something distinctly odd about Reverend Thingy-Thingy,' said Horatio, who always struggled with hyphenated surnames. 'My money's on him.'

'Not that you've *got* any money,' said Eustace. 'You fritter it all away on aniseed balls. But what do you mean, your money's on him?'

'That he's the one that did in the Colonel,' said Horatio. 'That's what I mean.'

Loveday shook her head. 'He's peculiar all right, I'll give you that. Just the sort of chap I'd write about in *Murder and Mayhem Magazine*. But I'd have to give him a motive first. And I can't think of a single reason why the Right Rev would want to put an end to the poor old Colonel.'

'Perhaps he didn't like people smoking pipes?' offered Master Oliver Davenport.

'Full marks for effort, old chap,' replied Eustace, with an encouraging nod. 'But if that were the case, the Reverend could have hidden the Colonel's pipe.

He didn't have to go to the trouble of biffing him over the head with a stuffed crow, now did he?' He sucked his lower lip, a thought slowly forming. 'I think we should be methodical about this, write a list of all the suspects and go through them one by one. There's just one thing I need to do first. You chaps go on up to the old nursery. I'll meet you there as soon as I can.'

'Why?' asked Horatio. 'Where are you going?'

'I need to check something in the library,' said Eustace. 'I'll catch you up.'

'I would go with you,' said Horatio, 'only it's a library. I'd quite happily pass a weekend here without clapping eyes on another book, let alone a whole room full of the things.'

—

Horatio, Loveday and Master Oliver Davenport continued along the hall on their way back to the old nursery wing. Outside, the howling gale had not let up and the branches of the horse chestnut trees were shaking violently.

'What's that, over there?' asked Master Oliver Davenport, looking out through a window and pointing across the windswept garden to a redbrick structure with a high domed roof. 'It looks like an igloo!'

'It's an ice-house,' explained Horatio. 'They used it in the olden days to store—'

'Ice?' suggested Master Oliver Davenport.

'Well, yes,' said Horatio. 'But they don't use it now, except to store the lawnmower.'

The rain was coming down heavily, lashing against the windows, and the children were relieved to return to the old nursery, where a fire had been lit. They made tea and waited for Eustace.

'How did you get on in the library?' asked Loveday when at last Eustace came through the door. 'Did you find whatever it was you were looking for?'

The boy smiled triumphantly, brandishing a copy of *Barrack's Encyclopaedia of Insect Life*. 'It was exactly as I thought,' he said. 'The creature in the Colonel's room is *Hottentotta tamulus*.' He opened the book and pointed to a large colour plate of the arachnid in question. 'There, you see? The Indian red scorpion!'

'And is it poisonous?' asked Loveday.

'Oh yes,' said Eustace. 'Deadly.'

'What does it matter what it's called?' said Horatio. 'Either it's deadly or it isn't … isn't it?'

Eustace turned to a map on the inside cover of the book. 'The fact that you've failed to grasp, my dear brother, is this. *Hottentotta tamulus* is a native of India, not Egypt.'

Master Oliver Davenport stared at Eustace in disbelief. 'You mean, the scorpion *didn't* come from Cairo at all?'

'That's exactly what I mean,' replied Eustace. 'And if it didn't come from Cairo, then somebody must have planted it in Colonel Theodore's room!'

'This is all simply ripping,' said Loveday. 'Though I'm sad that the Colonel's dead, of course. He was a potty sort of a person, but I'd have one of him to three hundred Great Aunt Henriettas.'

'You're right,' said Eustace. 'The Colonel was

a decent chap. The least we can do is unmask his killer, before that fool of an Inspector beats us to it.'

'Or Great Aunt Henrietta,' added Horatio.

Eustace took out his pocket notebook, and turned to a fresh page. 'We need to write out a list of suspects,' he said, licking the tip of his pencil. 'We should start with everybody who was in the house yesterday.'

He began to write:

Suspects

Family/Guests	Staff
Aunt Maude	Cook
Uncle Max	Horton
Uncle Rufus	Percival
Great Aunt Henrietta	Violet
The Reverend	

'Well, Cook can't have done it, for a start,' said Horatio, who trusted the innocence of anyone who fed him well. 'She's an absolute pet. And besides, she makes the most mouth-watering jam roly-poly pudding I've ever tasted in my life.'

But Eustace shook his head. 'We have to be logical and methodical at all times in our investigations,' he said. 'We can't allow our thoughts to become muddied by affection, family allegiance or jam roly-poly pudding. Cook must stay on the list until we're quite certain that she's innocent of the crime.' He snapped his notebook shut. 'Now, we must begin our inquiries.'

'Who shall we question first?' asked Loveday.

'Uncle Rufus, I think,' said Eustace. 'After all, he did say how wonderful it would be if a murder took place at Bleakley Manor. It seems his wish came true.'

Chapter Seven

Reckless Uncle Rufus

THE CHILDREN DISCOVERED Uncle Rufus in the smoking room, busily helping himself to cigars from Sir Max's humidor.

'Come in and close the door,' he said, hastily stuffing a fistful of cigars into his trouser pocket. 'I don't want that inspector catching up with me again until I've got a scotch and soda inside me. To steady the nerves, you understand.'

Loveday peered out into the passageway. When she was quite certain that the coast was clear, she quietly pushed the door shut.

'Prowling round the hallowed halls as if he owns the place,' continued Uncle Rufus. 'He reminds me of the gnats that buzz over the marsh in the heat of summer. You'd need two of him to make an actual policeman. I don't just mean in height, I mean in brainpower. I have a grave suspicion that there isn't much going on inside that benighted noggin of his.'

'You seem very calm about matters,' said Eustace. 'Considering there's been a murder this morning.'

'Oh, you know me,' said Uncle Rufus, smoothing his hair with the palm of his hand, 'always hankering after a bit of excitement to jolly things along, what? I wonder how the murderer plans to kill his next victim?'

Master Oliver Davenport gave a shudder and Uncle Rufus grinned wickedly at him.

'What makes you think there *will* be another murder?' asked Eustace.

'Well, you know,' said Uncle Rufus, 'just a hunch, I suppose. Bleakley Manor's ripe with likely victims. Defenestrated ... that would be a devilish way to despatch a foe. Propelling him through an open window and down, down on to the cold, hard ground below.'

He grinned again and lit one of the stolen cigars. 'I always think that must be a frightful way to go!'

'We do have some questions for you, Uncle Rufus,' said Horatio, as Eustace took out his pocket notebook and sharpened his pencil to a perfect point.

'Then ask away, niece and nephews all,' replied Uncle Rufus. He nodded in the direction of Master Oliver Davenport. 'And the same goes for Poor Unfortunates, whomsoever they may be. I daresay you'll do a better job of solving the crime than that fool of an Inspector. To get the ball rolling I might as well confess to a little cigar looting, what?' Failing to locate an ashtray, he tapped the end of his cigar into the wastepaper basket.

Loveday settled herself on a footstool as Eustace turned the pages of his notebook.

'This should be fun,' continued Uncle Rufus, reclining languidly in an armchair. 'Let the interrogation begin!' His eyes twinkled mischievously. 'Although looking at Loveday, I'm rather surprised your little gang has come down on the side of the law.'

Choosing to ignore his uncle's quip, Eustace took a deep breath and began his questioning. 'You won't deny that you were snooping through Sir Max's personal and private papers,' he said, hoping to catch Uncle Rufus off-guard.

'Now look here,' protested the uncle, 'you're not pinning the murder on me, are you? I'll freely admit to pinching a cigar or twelve, but biffing the Colonel over the head? Well, that's another matter entirely.' Loveday reached for the soda siphon to extinguish the flames that were now licking from the wastepaper basket. Uncle Rufus frowned. 'How did you know I'd been searching through Max's papers anyway?'

'It was a theory of mine,' replied Eustace. 'It seemed strange that you reached under the desk and found the will. I couldn't understand why you didn't let the Inspector discover it for himself. You didn't find it there at all, did you? You were returning it before it was missed.'

'Yes,' said Uncle Rufus, unabashed by this

revelation. 'You're quite right, of course. But let's keep it between these four walls.' He indicated the walls airily with his hand, dropping ash from the cigar and singeing the carpet. 'Max had threatened to change his will. I wanted to see if he'd put his threat into action.'

'But you're only his brother-in-law,' said Eustace. 'Why did you expect to inherit anything?'

'The old skinflint had cut the Colonel out,' said Uncle Rufus. 'But Maudy's still going to do rather well when Sir Max pops his clogs. And my dear sister does dote on me. She'd buy me any motorcar I wanted … I'd simply have to click my fingers.' His fringe flopped down over his left eye and he smoothed it back into place. 'I imagine that's what you might call a motive.' He smiled broadly at the children. 'And I suppose you think I crept into the study in the dead of night to hurry things along, what?'

'Unless the killer wasn't planning to kill Sir Max in the first place?' said Loveday.

Uncle Rufus raised his eyebrows. 'You mean

the Colonel may have been the intended victim all along?' Wrong-footed by the directness of Loveday's comment, he stubbed out the cigar on the rim of the wastepaper basket. 'I was rather fond of the old loony, as a matter of fact. What reason would I have for seeing him off?'

Wishing he could conjure up a motive, Eustace gave an anxious cough.

Uncle Rufus smiled and nodded his head. 'Any more questions?' he asked, as Loveday extinguished the smouldering cigar butt with another squirt from the soda siphon. 'Or am I a free man?'

'For now,' said Eustace. 'Though we should probably report you for the theft of Uncle Max's cigars.'

Uncle Rufus laughed though he was clearly shaken. 'So, it's like that, is it?' he said and held out his wrists. 'Clap me in irons then. I'll come quietly, m'lud.'

'We'll take no further action if you return them now,' said Eustace firmly.

'Very well,' said the uncle, petulantly thrusting his hand into his pocket to recover the ill-gotten gains and returning them to the cigar humidor.

'We'll speak no more of it,' said Eustace, gravely. 'But remember, Uncle, a life of crime never pays.'

'Very good,' said Uncle Rufus. Downcast, he departed empty-handed and empty-pocketed, creeping away as stealthily as a cat burglar.

'Crime never pays?' whispered Horatio to his brother. 'Where did you get that from?'

'It was rather ripe stuff, wasn't it?' said Eustace, his face breaking into a smile. 'I read it in a detective novel once. I might even use it again if I get the chance!'

Loveday was scowling out of the window, watching as Inspector Hanwell searched for clues among the rhododendron bushes.

'What's up now, cuz?' asked Horatio.

'It's the Inspector,' grunted Loveday. 'Sticking his big fat nose into our business.'

'Then we should go and search the Colonel's

room,' said Eustace with a sly grin, 'while the Inspector's safely out of our way.'

—

'Do you suppose the murderer was trying to steal something from in here?' asked Loveday, as the children searched carefully through Colonel Theodore's now deserted room. 'One of the nose-harp thingies, do you think? Maybe the Colonel caught him in the act and that's why he was done in?'

'Nobody's going to pay good money for a Grecian nose harp,' said Horatio, 'no matter how ancient it is.' He shuddered to see the scorpion, now skewered to the wall with a long copper pin. 'And anyway, if Colonel Theodore *had* caught someone attempting to steal something, wouldn't he have been biffed over the head in here, rather than in Uncle Max's study? Don't you think, Eustace?'

But Eustace was not listening. His curiosity had been aroused by a small pile of terracotta dust that had collected on the floor by the fireplace. 'Interesting,' he said, crouching down and rubbing the coarse dust between finger and thumb.

'Do you think it's coming down the chimney?' asked Loveday.

'I don't think it's brick dust,' said Eustace, smearing a sample on a blank page of his pocket notebook. 'It looks older than that, somehow.' He noticed a small piece of paper protruding from beneath the rug and pulled it out.

'What've you got there?' asked Loveday.

Eustace held out the paper. On it were these words:

THEODORE – MEET ME IN MY
STUDY AT 10 PM
MAX

'Curiouser and curiouser,' observed Eustace. 'I think we should pay Uncle Max a visit and ask him about this note. Now buck up, you lot, there's detecting to do.'

Chapter Eight

Quite the Perfect Pickle

THE CHILDREN KNOCKED at the door of Sir Max's study. The door opened and Sir Max appeared, his eyes burning with a ghoulish intensity. 'Ever seen a marrow like this?' he cooed with a fatherly smile, cradling the vegetable like a babe in arms; a babe that was shortly to be pulped and pickled. He ushered the children inside. 'I knew you couldn't stay away for long. The tragic death of my brother has been unsettling for you all,' he observed, gesturing the chalk outline on the floor, 'and in times of need your minds have understandably turned to pickling for solace.' He handed a folded cardboard chart to each of the children. 'The colour of each and every one of my hundred and fifty varieties of pickle and table sauce,' he declared proudly and opened a large cupboard door behind his desk, revealing jars and bottles of his favourite pickles and sauces. Eustace glanced along a shelf.

No. 12.   HORSERADISH SAVOURY

No. 37.   BENGAL HOT CHUTNEY

No. 56.   SPICED TOMATO RELISH

No. 89.   GHERKIN AND CAPERBERRY
PIQUANT PICKLE

No. 101. ESSENCE OF OYSTER

No. 111. FINEST CUMBERLAND SAUCE
'THE EPICUREAN'

No. 120. TOMATO AND CAPSICUM
RELISH

No. 147. EMPIRE ANCHOVY SAUCE

Sir Max took down a bottle of pickle from the shelf. 'Number One – Mustard Piccalilli, as bright and golden as the summer sun,' he observed in a hushed tone. He turned to Master Oliver Davenport, snatched up an onion from his desk and waved it in the air. 'Know what this is, boy?'

'It is an onion, sir,' answered Master Oliver Davenport with some confidence. For though he was a Poor Unfortunate, he was not so poor and unfortunate that he had never crossed paths with the vegetable in question.

'Quite correct,' said Sir Max. 'I like a boy who knows his onions,' he added and laughed at his own joke. 'Give a boy an onion and he has nothing. But give a boy an onion and a spoonful of mustard powder and he has the makings of a jar of piccalilli.'

'Actually, Uncle Max—' began Eustace.

Sir Max was not to be interrupted and he shook the onion violently to silence the boy. 'But that's not all,' he continued. 'A whole cucumber goes into a jar of piccalilli. That surprises a good many people, don't-you-know? "Cucumbers, pah!" they say. But without cucumber a mustard piccalilli is not a mustard piccalilli. And good malt vinegar, that's the ticket! Stir it all up and leave it a goodish while and that's how you make a mustard piccalilli.'

Eustace gave a polite but significant cough.

'What is it, boy?' boomed Sir Max.

'I'm afraid we didn't come to talk to you about piccalilli, sir,' said Eustace.

Sir Max's manner changed in an instant; his eyes narrowed to slits and his voice cracked with barely contained anger. 'You mean you're *not* here because of pickles?'

'No, sir,' said Eustace.

'Not any variety of pickle at all?'

'No, sir,' said Eustace, taking a step backwards as his uncle slowly advanced on him. 'Actually, we have some questions for you.'

'Then out with it, out with it!' snapped Sir Max. 'State your business and be quick about it!'

'We wanted to ask you about Colonel Theodore,' said Horatio.

'And whether you might have an alibi for the time of the murder,' added Loveday.

Master Oliver Davenport held up the pickling chart as Sir Max's face changed colour suddenly from No. 12 Horseradish Savoury to No. 56 Spiced Tomato Relish.

Sir Max's voice dropped to a resonant rumble. 'An alibi?' he growled. 'I had nothing to do with my brother's death. I was working in my secret pickling laboratory, experimenting with a new variety of mango chutney ...' He stopped, his temper evaporating in the blink of an eye. 'Don't tell your aunt I told you that,' he pleaded. 'I promised her I wouldn't pickle, you see. Not over the Michaelmas weekend.'

'So Aunt Maude didn't know?' said Horatio.

Sir Max uttered a plaintive cry. 'She has no love for pickling! She doesn't even know my laboratory exists!'

'If you had nothing to do with Colonel Theodore's death then how do you explain this?' asked Eustace, producing the note they had found in the Colonel's room.

'I've never seen that in my life!' said Sir Max, his moustache twitching more violently than ever. 'Now get out of my study and leave me in peace with my marrow!'

'What do you make of that?' asked Loveday, as they left Sir Max's study. 'I knew Uncle Max was a bit of a crackpot, but secret pickling laboratories? Cripes!'

Eustace was recording his observations in his pocket notebook.

> *Uncle Max, a man of quick temper, who loves vegetables more than his own family. Quite possibly the murderous type. Is there really a pickling laboratory, or is it merely a figment of his vinegar-addled imagination?*

'Most decidedly strange,' he observed as he closed the notebook. 'I think it's time to go and talk to Aunt Maude, don't you?'

They found Aunt Maude looking pale and

dishevelled in the hallway. 'You must stay in the house for the rest of the day,' she commanded. 'It's too dangerous to wander out on to the lawn in this weather. Though I doubt you're any safer indoors. It wouldn't surprise me if we are left here alone until every last one of us is dead.'

Loveday gazed out from a window. The rain was thundering against the gravel drive and water gurgled down the lead drainpipes, yet in the distance she could see that Great Aunt Henrietta had thrown caution to the wind and was striding purposefully across the lawn. She was pursued at a distance by the Reverend Edwin Saline-Crum. The Great Aunt, shod in sturdy walking boots, was making short work of her post-breakfast stroll. The Reverend, however, was struggling to stop his shoes from sinking into the boggy lawn. A moment later they were both swallowed up by the swirling mist.

'Did you have any reason to wish Colonel Theodore dead, Aunt Maude?' asked Eustace, believing that a direct approach often produced the best results with a vague relative.

It was obvious that the question had unsettled Aunt Maude and she gave her nephew a reproachful glare. 'If I had a reason, I'm sure I would remember.'

'And can you remember?' asked Horatio.

'No,' replied Aunt Maude haughtily. ' I cannot.'

Before the children could ask another question, the front door burst open and in trudged a miserable-looking Inspector Hanwell, trailing muddy footprints behind him. Horton, who had appeared as if from thin air, attempted to remain in front of the Inspector, laying sheets of newspaper on the polished floor for the man to step on.

'Try not to drop any more mud!' commanded Aunt Maude. 'You really should have stayed inside, Inspector. You might have been struck by lightning or … or worse.'

The Inspector's clothes had shrunk in the rain and the cuffs of his shirt had become so tight that his hands were slowly turning blue. 'I fell in the nettles,' he said weakly. 'I got stung all over.'

Aunt Maude frowned. 'And what on earth were you doing in the nettles in the first place, might I ask?'

'I wasn't *in* the nettles,' said the Inspector. 'I told you … I *fell into* the nettles. I was seeing if there were any footprints leading through the flowerbeds to the study window.'

'Horton,' said Aunt Maude, 'fetch me a bottle of calamine lotion to rub on the Inspector's nettle rash.'

'I'm not going to be rubbing on calamine lotion with them children stood there gawping,' said the Inspector.

'Very well,' sighed Aunt Maude and turned to Horton. 'Take him to the nearest bathroom and make sure he cleans himself thoroughly. His clothes are beyond washing, I think. We shall have to burn them.'

The Inspector's face dropped. 'Burn my clothes?' he moaned. 'You can't burn my clothes!'

'I don't think the Inspector is quite tall enough to fit into Eustace's clothes,' said Aunt Maude, ignoring the man's protests. 'Perhaps we can dress him in something of Horatio's?'

'Oh yes,' grinned Horatio. 'He can help himself.' He turned to the Inspector. 'I do sometimes leave half-sucked toffees and aniseed balls and things in my pockets, though. So do be prepared.'

'Do you have any suspects in mind yet?' asked Loveday, thinking it doubtful that much was going on inside the Inspector's mind at all.

'I don't trust that footman for a start,' said the Inspector. 'First thing I said to him, he clammed up like an oyster.'

'Or rather, he clammed up like a clam,' suggested Eustace and Loveday let out an involuntary gulp of laughter.

'You think you're clever, don't you?' said the Inspector.

'My school report bears testament to the fact,' answered Eustace. 'Perhaps you would care to read it, Inspector? I'm top of the form in English and Algebra and—'

'I think it's time to go, Eustace,' said Horatio,

pulling his brother by the arm and leading him away before the Inspector could erupt in anger.

'Yes, children, that's quite enough,' agreed Aunt Maude. 'Now, please stop asking impertinent questions and make yourselves useful. The silver dish for the Michaelmas pie needs to be fetched from upstairs. Perhaps that would better occupy your energy.'

———

'Maybe your aunt's just pretending to be so forgetful?' suggested Master Oliver Davenport, as they set off upstairs to collect the silver pie dish.

Eustace regarded the boy wryly. 'Then she's been pretending all her life,' he said.

'She's so absentminded,' said Horatio, 'she might very well have bumped off the Colonel then forgotten all about it!'

Horatio led the way to the west wing of the house and up a winding oak staircase into one of the turrets, with Loveday, Eustace and Master Oliver Davenport following behind. 'The dish is kept in here,' he announced, arriving at a doorway surmounted by two crossed pikes. 'The Bleakley family museum. It's full to the rafters with grisly relics!' He turned the iron handle and pushed hard against the heavy door, which he then propped open with a cannonball that had been provided for such a purpose.

It was a cold, whitewashed room which housed the assorted curios of the Bleakley family that had been collected over the centuries. It was a museum without order. There was a stone gargoyle with a cracked nose that had long ago fallen from the roof of the house; a wooden tray with clay pipes in shattered pieces; a collection of porcelain inkwells; copper hunting horns; false teeth in tin cases; early mantraps that had once ensnared unwary poachers; and ancient iron keys to doors unknown and unknowable. And everything smelled of dust.

'Those swords are from the Civil War,' said Master Oliver Davenport, pointing to a wall of the turret, where armoury and weaponry hung in abundance. 'I've been reading about the olden times at school, you see.'

'Half of the family were Cavaliers and supported the king,' said Horatio, feeling around inside a rusting helmet and dredging up a handful of musket balls. 'The other half were Roundheads and wanted to chop the king's head off. The Bleakleys can't agree on anything, especially when it comes to warfare and bloodshed.'

A crow idly tapped its beak against the windowpane and drew the children's attention to a large sackcloth head that hung from two iron hooks set high up on the wall. The head was stuffed with straw and horsehair and the mouth was sewn shut with twine. It seemed to leer down at them, a thing of nightmares.

'Feast your eyes on that,' said Horatio. 'Old Bramble Head in the flesh!'

Master Oliver Davenport retreated in alarm, his back pressing against the plastered wall of the museum; it was damp and clammy, as though the room had absorbed water like a sponge.

'Not the *real* Old Bramble Head, of course,' corrected Eustace, hardly bringing himself to look up at the face. 'Only a costume. In days of yore a servant would dress up, wearing that head, to scare away any evil spirits that might have collected in the house since the previous Michaelmas celebrations. The tradition goes back at least four centuries.'

Turning away from the grinning visage of Old Bramble Head, Master Oliver Davenport peered into a large glass case and was greeted by a most peculiar sight. Against a small curtain of red velvet stood a grisly gathering of stuffed hamsters, each dressed in tailcoat and black bow tie. One of the hamsters held a pair of opera glasses to his eyes, while another was posed as if raising his silk top hat. Below the case, a strip of yellowing paper bore the legend:

A Night at the Opera.

'A little morbid,' said Master Oliver Davenport, leaning so close to the case that his breath fogged the glass. 'I wonder if they died and then they were stuffed, or was it the other way round?'

'This is rather fun though,' said Horatio, pointing at a pair of duelling pistols in a wooden case. 'They belonged to Giffard and Fortescue Bleakley nearly two hundred years ago. They fought a duel together. One brother lost an arm and the other lost a foot. The carved replacements are displayed here!' He reached up and set the wooden foot swinging on its iron hook like the pendulum of a clock, laughing as it kicked against the wooden arm with a sound like the rattling of old bones.

'What became of them?' asked Master Oliver Davenport.

'They died tragically, of course,' said Horatio. 'That's generally what happens with us Bleakleys. Bad case of woodworm.'

Master Oliver Davenport stared in bewilderment.

'He's joking,' said Loveday. 'Honestly, you're such an ass sometimes, Horatio.'

'And that,' said Eustace, gesturing grandly to a large wooden board, which hung above a long-abandoned fireplace, 'is the recipe for the famous blackberry pie, eaten by the Bleakley family every Michaelmas Day for over three hundred years.'

Master Oliver Davenport gazed up as directed and attempted to fathom out the writing:

The year of our Lord 1625

To make a goodly pye for the festivale of Michaelmas. Gather up ye berryes and an apple, cored. Put in butter, sugar and spice. Work them with ye back of a spoon and make it be thikke. Take a dyshe and lay in a crust of good sweet paste and more paste to cover it. Set ye to taske ornamenting this most excellente pye with trimming of paste made all to look of ye bramble and ye berryes. Pricke it all over till it be Owell prick'd. Make ye oven hot with coal and bake the pye till it be crisp and golden. Serve it up hot with ye cream, well sweetened. Leave not the remains of the pye past Michaelmas for fear that Old Bramble Head himself will come to taste of it.

Below the recipe, in another glass cabinet, was a deep silver dish engraved with blackberries and a tangle of brambles.

'Cook uses it every year,' said Horatio, opening the cabinet and taking out the dish. 'It's been handed down through generations of Bleakleys.'

'If the dish is as large as that then the pie must be absolutely *enormous*,' said Master Oliver Davenport, his eyes widening and his stomach growling hungrily at the thought.

———

Downstairs in the kitchen, Cook, Violet and Percival were busy with preparations for the Michaelmas feast. Horton was sitting in his pantry, in front of the open door of the enormous silver safe, polishing a vegetable tureen with a bottle of Silv-o-Shine.

Eustace could not help but notice as Percival leant forward to whisper in Violet's ear; the girl lowered her head, smiling and growing pink around the cheeks.

'Thirty years I've been here,' grumbled Cook,

'and I've never known a murder here in all that time. Terrible unexpected accidental deaths, yes … but murdering? No.'

'So you haven't killed anyone?' grinned Master Oliver Davenport.

'I haven't,' said Cook, then dropped her voice, 'though I won't tell a lie, there's been moments when I was sorely tempted.'

'Anyone in particular?' asked Loveday.

'That's for me to know,' said Cook mysteriously. 'Well,' she went on, 'standing here nattering won't get luncheon started. And then I've got the goose to prepare for dinner and the blackberry pie to make.'

'It's going to be the largest pie ever made!' laughed Master Oliver Davenport, as they handed over the silver dish. 'Enough to last for days and days!'

But Cook shook her finger at the boy. 'Everybody knows that Michaelmas Day is the last day we eat blackberries,' she said. 'Or else the very devil will come to spit on them. I don't know *what* they teach you at school these days.'

With a sudden rustling of tweed, Great Aunt Henrietta entered the kitchen. She watched disdainfully as Cook took two tins of lobster from the larder.

'Maude says we are to have lobster mayonnaise for lunch,' said the Great Aunt, fixing Cook with a forceful stare.

Cook appeared nonplussed by the arrival of the unexpected visitor, and in reply silently held up the tins of lobster.

'I won't beat about the bush,' continued the Great Aunt, her steely eyes glinting. 'On my last visit, the lobster mayonnaise was unsatisfactory. The mixture was too thin and tasted strongly of vinegar. Nobody knows how to make mayonnaise any more, so I will show you. Now, eggs. Bring me eggs!'

Without a word, Cook did as she was told and fetched the egg crate.

The Great Aunt rolled up her sleeves and cracked twelve egg yolks into the bowl. She added a stream of oil and a grinding of white pepper then whisked the ingredients with violent force. 'And how is your investigation going, Great Aunt Henrietta?' asked Eustace, crossing his fingers behind his back in the earnest hope that the answer would be 'very badly'.

If the Great Aunt was surprised to see the four children standing before her, she showed no delight at the discovery.

'My investigations are proceeding as expected,' she replied. 'I will reveal the identity of the murderer by the end of the day.'

Horatio let out an involuntary whimper of disappointment and the aged relative glowered in his direction.

When the mixture was thick enough to hold a fork upright, Great Aunt Henrietta returned the bowl to Cook. 'There,' she said, 'that is how to make a proper mayonnaise.'

Uncertain of what to say, Cook made a slight curtsy. The Great Aunt grunted and went on her way.

'Comes barging into my kitchen as if she owns

the place,' grumbled Cook as she opened the tins of lobster and mixed the contents with the Great Aunt's freshly made mayonnaise. 'Teaching me how to make mayonnaise, indeed! Did she teach her own grandmother to suck eggs? If ever a person deserved to meet a sticky end—' She stopped herself suddenly and her face coloured with embarrassment. 'Oh, whatever must you think of me?' she gushed. 'Talking out of turn like that about your Great Auntie. I'm so ashamed of myself.'

'Oh, it's all right,' said Horatio glumly, 'we're not terribly fond of her either.'

'Now get along with you,' said Cook, 'there's a goose to roast and a pie to bake and the dinner won't make itself, now will it?'

'It might all be bluster anyway,' said Horatio, as the children walked along the portrait corridor on their way upstairs. 'The Great Aunt could have bumped off the Colonel as easily as anybody else.'

'But she's an old woman,' said Master Oliver

Davenport. 'She couldn't have wielded a stuffed crow in anger.'

'Oh, couldn't she?' said Loveday. 'I didn't think so either, until I saw her downstairs in the kitchen. The way she whisked that mayonnaise for lunch! She must have muscles like Goliath. I think she could have wielded *two* stuffed crows if she'd wanted.'

'But with what possible motive?' asked Eustace, drawing a large question mark in his pocket notebook beside the Great Aunt's name.

'I don't know,' said Loveday. 'I don't think she liked the Colonel awfully much.'

Eustace sighed. 'If Great Aunt Henrietta killed everybody she didn't like, then we'd all be dead by now.'

Turning a corner, the children were startled to see Percival, lurking in the shadows.

'So, you're investigating the murder as well, is that it?' He smirked. 'You and that busybody Great Aunt of yours.' He sniffed and slouched away. 'A whole rotten family full of meddlers.'

Eustace pursed his lips. 'This should be a reminder,' he whispered, 'that children should be seen but not overheard.'

Chapter Nine

A Spectre at the Feast

AT SIX O'CLOCK in the evening the Bleakley family gathered in the hall, beneath the boughs of an ornamental apple tree, to exchange Michaelmas gifts. It seemed strange to Master Oliver Davenport that the celebrations were to continue despite Colonel Theodore's murder. However, to Eustace, Horatio and Loveday, no amount of unusual behaviour at Bleakley Manor was a surprise to them.

Eustace was still glumly contemplating Great Aunt Henrietta's claim that she was close to solving the murder of Colonel Theodore, so much so that it did not even raise a smile when he encountered Inspector Hanwell, dressed in Horatio's cast-off clothes – a pullover that was two sizes too large, and a pair of trousers so short that they revealed a good inch of bare leg, still pink from nettle stings and dabbed liberally with calamine lotion.

Uncle Max presented each of the children with a jar of his Special Reserve Piccalilli, which came in a small wooden crate complete with a porcelain spoon engraved with the crest of the Bleakley family.

There was a box of lavender bath cubes from Aunt Maude, a truckle of cheese from the Reverend Saline-Crum and a box of caviar puffs from Uncle Rufus. The Great Aunt gave them each an autographed copy of her latest novel, *Cursed by Day and Cursed by Night*. Inspector Hanwell, who had no gifts to give, greedily accepted the box of chocolate gingers presented to him by Aunt Maude.

Eustace, Horatio and Master Oliver Davenport exchanged bags of sweets and Loveday passed out handwritten luggage labels.

Horatio read his label. 'I.O.U one copy of *Murder and Mayhem Magazine*. Price, sixpence.'

'It's not a gift if you charge for it,' explained Eustace.

'I have to cover my costs,' said Loveday defensively.

Though Colonel Theodore was dead, he had left Michaelmas gifts for the children wrapped in the pages of old archaeological maps. There was a brass magnifying glass for Eustace, a compass of grey gunmetal for Horatio and, for Loveday, a terracotta bust of Thoth, the bird-headed Egyptian god of writing and knowledge. There was also a book on the history of hieroglyphics for Master Oliver Davenport. It was not labelled 'Orphan' or 'Poor Unfortunate', as was often the case, but instead 'Master Oliver Davenport'.

'I shall treasure it,' said the boy, slipping the book safely inside his pocket.

Percival lit the candles that lined the hall with a long wax taper and Horton lit the large Michaelmas candle that stood in a gilded holder beside the stuffed bear. When the hallway was aglow, Horton switched out the electric lights and Cook entered proudly from the kitchen, carrying the roast goose under a silver cover. Violet followed behind with an enormous tureen of sage and onion stuffing.

Finally, Sir Max and Aunt Maude led the guests in procession behind Cook and Violet, and the family sang the goose into the dining room. Master Oliver Davenport, who did not know the words, mouthed along like a goldfish.

Michaelmas daisies among wild weeds
Bloom for St Michael's valiant deeds
You slayed a dragon, killed it dead
Now save us from Old Bramble Head!

The dinner table was bedecked with silver candelabra and swags of trailing ivy, stuck about with fresh Michaelmas daisies. The family and guests took their seats as Cook lifted the silver cover from the dish to reveal the glistening goose, then gave a small curtsy.

Sir Max remained standing to carve the enormous

bird. 'Aunt Henrietta?'

'I'll have the dark meat,' replied the Great Aunt, as Violet filled her glass with lemon barley water. 'The neck.'

Sir Max set to work carving the meat and Horton carried round a dish of apple sauce.

The Reverend Saline-Crum was preparing to say grace, when Great Aunt Henrietta climbed to her feet. 'Now that we are all gathered here,' she began, 'I must tell you that I have solved the mystery of Theodore's murder. And as soon as we have eaten, I will reveal the truth.' Without uttering another word, she sat down.

'The old girl's finally lost her marbles,' whispered Uncle Rufus to Master Oliver Davenport. 'The beetroot's gone to her brainbox!'

A ripple of murmured conversation passed around the dinner table. Sir Max and Aunt Maude exchanged anxious glances, and the Reverend Saline-Crum's eyes stuck out further than ever. Inspector Hanwell, who had nearly inhaled a slice of boiled potato as

Great Aunt Henrietta made her speech, was now glowering malevolently at his rival, and grinding his teeth slowly together.

Loveday leaned across to Eustace. 'Do you think she *really* knows?' she whispered.

'I don't doubt it,' replied Eustace, who had suddenly lost his appetite. 'And all our investigations will have been for nothing.'

When the assembled company had served themselves with apple sauce, Horton gave a discreet cough. 'Will that be all, sir?'

Sir Max waved the carving knife. 'Thank you, Horton,' he said. 'We will ring for the pie.'

Horton gave a bow and retired from the room. Violet remained, hovering uncertainly by the sideboard, wine decanter in hand.

The atmosphere at the dinner table was sombre. The Reverend Saline-Crum, who was seated beside the Great Aunt and had broken out in a cold sweat, talked endlessly about his missionary work in East Africa, and Sir Max discussed the advantages and disadvantages of varieties of pickling vinegar. Loveday, who had smuggled Pineapple Cube into the dining room hidden in a silver evening purse, took every opportunity to reach beneath the table to feed the rat with slices of goose and boiled potato.

All the time the Inspector chewed noisily. Aunt Maude frowned and rattled her pearl necklace distractedly. It finally proved too much for her. 'Please be good enough not to chew with your mouth open, Inspector,' she hissed.

Inspector Hanwell scowled at Aunt Maude, but closed his mouth even so and chewed on silently.

The wind howled banshee-like around the solid brick walls of Bleakley Manor and the tips of the longest branches tapped against the windowpanes, like unseen hands clawing at the glass. Mustard and Pickle padded listlessly around the room, as if afraid of their own shadows.

When the goose had been polished off and it was time to bring in the blackberry pie, Aunt Maude rang the electric bell.

But Horton did not appear.

'Most peculiar,' said Aunt Maude. 'Butlers don't simply disappear into thin air, do they?'

'Watkins did,' whispered Horatio, exchanging a knowing glance with Eustace.

Uncle Rufus reached across and started tapping out Morse code on the bell. 'S.O.S.,' he grinned. 'Save Our Supper, what?'

The Great Aunt tutted, her chin shiny with goose fat. She reached for her goblet of lemon barley water and took a deep gulp.

'Quiet,' commanded Aunt Maude, as Pickle uttered a low growl and backed away from the door.

Mustard started yelping too and retreated beneath the dining table.

'What on earth is the matter with them?' asked Aunt Maude, turning in bewilderment to Sir Max, who seemed equally baffled by the behaviour of the two dogs.

'Ma'am …' murmured Violet, a trembling finger pointing to the door.

The handle was slowly turning and the children watched open-mouthed and dumbfounded as a strange figure, with long arms like pitchforks and a head of sackcloth, entered the room in short, jerking steps.

'Old Bramble Head!' gasped Sir Max.

Loveday turned to her cousins, unsure whether to laugh or cry out in alarm.

The figure shuffled towards the dinner table, trailing straw and horsehair as it moved. The pitchfork arms were outstretched as it stalked forward, looming over the Great Aunt before moving off round the table and departing from the dining room the same way it had come.

'Well, that was quite a lark!' grinned Uncle Rufus. 'Bringing Old Bramble Head back to life!'

'I suppose that was all your doing, Rufus?' said Great Aunt Henrietta, removing a bramble thorn from her glass that had fallen from the outstretched claws of the unbidden guest. She motioned to Violet, who approached with a second decanter of lemon barley water and filled the Great Aunt's glass.

'It's nothing to do with me,' laughed Uncle Rufus. 'It must be Horton, entering into the spirit of things, what? That explains why he hasn't brought the pie in.'

'You mean ...' said Master Oliver Davenport, letting out a long-held breath, 'that it wasn't *really* Old Bramble Head?'

Horatio got up from his chair on trembling legs. He walked towards the door and peered out into the hall.

'Well?' barked Sir Max. 'What can you see?'

'There's no one out there,' said Horatio, straining his eyes to see in the shadowy passageway. 'No one at all.'

The Great Aunt grasped her goblet and raised it to her lips. 'This is not the moment for amateur theatricals,' she said and turned to Sir Max. 'If my servants behaved in such a manner, I would cast them out of the house at once.' She took a long sip of her lemon barley water then slammed the goblet back down on the table.

As she did so, her eyes seemed to glaze – she slumped forward, gave a single convulsive shudder, and lay still and silent.

'A jolly peculiar place to catch forty winks,' said Uncle Rufus uncertainly. 'That's what I say.'

The Reverend Saline-Crum turned slowly in his chair and held his fingers to the Great Aunt's throat.

'Is she dead?' asked Loveday.

'Of course she's not dead,' said Aunt Maude with feeling.

Master Oliver Davenport leaned forward in his chair so he could get a better look. 'I think she is.'

'Please don't contradict, dear,' said Aunt Maude.

'The boy is quite correct,' said the Reverend, who seemed suddenly less anxious than he had been all weekend. 'The unfortunate lady is indeed dead.'

Aunt Maude gulped so hard that her pearl choker rattled.

'She meddled and she was bletted,' whispered Master Oliver Davenport.

'Poor Auntie,' said Sir Max, who looked stricken at the death of his aged relative. 'All that steamed beetroot, I shouldn't wonder. That's what did it for her. I must have told her a hundred times that beetroot is far superior when pickled.'

Inspector Hanwell held up the Great Aunt's goblet and sniffed hard. 'Bitter almonds,' he said. 'It wasn't the beetroot that got her, it was the lemon barley water. Someone's been and poisoned the old woman with cyanide!' He advanced on the Reverend Saline-Crum. 'Was it you?' he demanded. 'You were sitting close enough to tip the stuff into her glass!'

'I ... I don't know what you mean,' stammered the Reverend as he loosened his dog collar. 'I never met the woman before I arrived at Bleakley Manor!' he croaked. 'What possible motive could I have had for wishing the woman harm?'

'We'll see,' said the Inspector, stalking from the dining room and along the hall. He made his way quickly down to the kitchen, closely pursued by Aunt Maude, Sir Max, Uncle Rufus and the

Reverend Saline-Crum. Violet followed behind with the children, her eyes bloodshot and fearful.

Cook was slumped across the kitchen table, the blackberry pie in front of her, untouched in its silver dish.

'They've killed Cook!' gasped Horatio.

'I don't think so,' said Loveday. 'Look, she's still breathing.'

'Oh, my poor aching head,' murmured Cook, slowly stirring and climbing to her feet. 'I feel like somebody's been and hit me with a lump hammer.'

The Inspector picked up Cook's teacup and sniffed hard. 'Just as I thought,' he said. 'Drugged.'

'That cup was left for me on the table,' said Cook, holding her hands to her head as she lowered herself back into the chair. 'I thought Violet had made it up for me. She's hopeless with custard, but she knows a thing or two about tea. It tasted bitter and I thought … well, I don't know what I thought. The next thing I knew I woke up to see you all standing there.'

Eustace stepped towards the table but Inspector

Hanwell held up his hand.

'Now don't you be getting your dirty paw marks all over my evidence,' he warned the boy. 'I'll be dusting for prints.'

Eustace opened his mouth to speak.

'And before you tell me there won't be any fingerprints,' said the Inspector quickly, 'I'll tell you this much for nothing – murderers is sloppy sometimes. And murderers makes mistakes sometimes. So there.' He rocked backwards and forwards on his feet, taking in the scene around him. 'This is a fine pickle, I must say.'

'Pickles, is it?' barked Sir Max.

'That's only my manner of speaking, sir,' said the Inspector hurriedly, cutting Sir Max off before he could begin listing ingredients. 'Now, who had a motive for killing the woman? That's what I want to know.'

'Everybody had a motive,' snorted Uncle Rufus. 'Nobody could stand the old windbag.'

'That a confession then, is it, sir?' asked the Inspector.

'Of course it's not a confession,' shot back Uncle Rufus. 'It's a simple statement of fact.'

From inside Horton's pantry there came a muffled moan. 'There's somebody in there!' cried Horatio, running quickly to the open door. It was a small room, with a roll-top desk and a chair. Built into the back wall of the pantry was the large green metal door of the 'PATENTED AIRTIGHT SILVER SAFE'. He pulled hard at the handle but the door would not give. 'There's no key!'

Horton's voice called weakly from inside the safe. 'There's a key in my tailcoat pocket, Master Horatio. Please hurry. There isn't much air left!'

The tailcoat hung from the back of Horton's chair and Horatio found the key in the inside breast pocket. 'I've got it!' he called. He unlocked the door and Horton staggered out from inside, gasping for breath.

'You could have been suffocated,' said Loveday as Uncle Rufus helped Horton out into the kitchen. 'Then that would have been two dead bodies in a single evening!'

Horton stared at the girl in bewilderment. '*Two* dead bodies?' he croaked.

'Great Aunt Henrietta,' explained Eustace. 'She's been poisoned.'

'I'll make a fresh pot of tea,' said Cook, swinging the kettle on to the stove. 'There's few things in this life that aren't put to rights by a good brew.'

Horton's legs seemed to buckle beneath him. 'He needs something stronger than tea,' said Sir Max. 'Have a tot of brandy, man. That'll see you right.'

'Did you get a good look at whoever done it?' asked Inspector Hanwell impatiently, as Cook poured out a glassful of brandy.

'*Did it*,' corrected Aunt Maude, with an impatient click of her tongue.

'I am most terribly sorry, Inspector,' mumbled Horton, staring miserably at the floor. 'I'm afraid I did not. Whoever it was, he shoved me in and pushed the door shut behind me.'

'So it *was* a man?' asked Loveday.

'I imagine so, miss,' said Horton, taking a large

gulp of the brandy. 'He pushed me so violently that I was almost knocked to the ground.'

'When exactly did this happen?' asked Eustace.

'I'll ask the questions, thank you very much,' said the Inspector, with a frown. He cleared his throat. 'When exactly did this happen?'

Horton took another sip of brandy. 'As soon as I came down from serving the goose, sir,' he replied.

'There's only one person unaccounted for,' said Sir Max, glancing around the room. 'And that's the footman, what's his name?'

'Percival,' offered Loveday, and Violet uttered a loud squeak of dismay.

'He is an unsavoury character,' said Horton. 'Pieces of silverware have gone missing. I'm most terribly sorry, Sir Max. I had hoped to keep the matter from you and deal with it myself.' He shook his head. 'I discovered that the man had been in prison for stealing silver from his previous employer. He assured me he was a reformed character and I always believe in giving a man a second chance. But now murder as well ...'

'I always suspected him,' said the Inspector with a grim smile of satisfaction. 'From the moment I first clapped eyes on the man I knew he was trouble. I daresay the Colonel and the old lady caught him pilfering and got murdered for their meddling. He must've locked the butler in the silver safe, drugged the cook, poisoned the lemon barley water, then made good his escape dressed as this Old Bramble Head character. We should sound the alarm!'

'The telephone lines are down,' said Sir Max. 'Or had you forgotten that? The man won't get far. There's no way across the bridge now, and if he tries to make it over the marsh then that's an end to the wretched individual.'

Violet let out a loud sob, mopping her eyes with the hem of her apron.

Horatio was puzzling over the chain of events; something did not quite seem to add up. 'But why did he only drug Cook?' he whispered to Eustace. 'Why didn't he drug Horton as well? Wouldn't it have been easier than locking him in the silver safe?'

The Inspector had opened the door of the meat larder and was surveying the game birds that hung from iron hooks in the low ceiling. 'There's nothing for it,' he said. 'We'll have to put the bodies in here to keep them fresh.'

Cook was beside herself. 'I've never heard of such a thing,' she wailed, wringing her hands. 'You're not putting corpses in the meat larder!'

'I'll put corpses where I want to put corpses!' said the Inspector.

'Not in my kitchen, you won't,' said Cook firmly. 'It was bad enough you leaving the Colonel wrapped up in the scullery. If you must leave bodies somewhere then you can carry them outside and put them in the old ice house.'

'Very well,' said the Inspector grudgingly.

'It seems one can hardly turn around without tripping over some corpse or other,' said Uncle Rufus, rolling his eyes. 'It's all so bothersome, isn't it?'

Sir Max glanced pointedly at his brother-in-law.

'You were the blighter with an appetite for murder, Rufus.'

The Inspector's ears pricked up. 'What's that you say, sir? Withholding evidence is a very serious matter. Very serious indeed.'

Uncle Rufus spoke before Sir Max could utter another word. 'What I meant was, my dear chap,' he began in the most withering voice he could muster, 'it's a tiresome house, stuffed to the rafters with tiresome people, and the prospect of some tedious blighter getting bumped off in the dead of night seemed entirely desirable to me.' He turned to the Inspector. 'Fingerprint me if you like,' he said. 'Examine my earthly goods and chattels. Leave no stone unturned. I've nothing to hide.' He struck a match and lit a cigarette.

'There'll be time enough for searching and the like, sir,' said Inspector Hanwell. 'But right now, I'm pressing you into service.'

Uncle Rufus blinked hard. 'And what, pray tell, do you mean by that?'

'The body wants moving,' said the Inspector, prodding Uncle Rufus in the chest. 'And *you're* going to help me move it.'

'Now wait one bally minute ...' protested Uncle Rufus.

But the Inspector was adamant and led the way back upstairs to the dining room with the family following behind. Master Oliver Davenport, who could show great presence of mind in testing times, took the blackberry pie with him.

The Great Aunt was a large woman and it took many minutes for Uncle Rufus and Inspector Hanwell to drag the body from the dining room and across the sodden lawn to the ice house.

'For all the good the Inspector did, I might as well have dragged her there by myself,' grumbled Uncle Rufus, returning from his unpleasant task. 'It turns out that the long arm of the law is nothing of the kind. At least Colonel Theodore was lighter. We should use the bally wheelbarrow next time we have to transport a body from A to B.'

'And are we expecting any more bodies?' asked Sir Max, glancing in horror at the Inspector.

'It pays to think ahead,' said Uncle Rufus.

'It's unhygienic,' lamented Aunt Maude. 'And isn't it true that dead bodies attract rats? It's quite bad enough to have two corpses about the place, but I will not have rats.'

It was unfortunate that at precisely that moment, Pineapple Cube made his bid for freedom. He leapt from Loveday's purse and scampered across the dining table towards the Michaelmas pie.

'You see?' moaned Aunt Maude, as Pineapple Cube landed heavily on the pie, cracking the pastry crust and sinking fast into the blackberry filling. 'I told you there'd be vermin!'

Master Oliver Davenport let out a howl of dismay.

'My Michaelmas pie!' shrieked Cook, flicking at the rat with the end of a tea towel.

'That's Pineapple Cube,' explained Loveday, darting across the room and lifting the sticky creature from the pie dish. 'He's my pet rat. It turns out it's a lot more difficult to train a rat than I thought.'

'I will not have rats!' cried Aunt Maude, steadying herself against a chair.

'He's an indoors sort of rat, really,' said Loveday. 'Not the plague-bringing type. Nothing to worry about.'

'Get it out!' shrieked Aunt Maude.

The fire had been made up in the old nursery in the east wing and the children gathered on the hearthrug. As they had been deprived of blackberry pie, they made up for this with slices of bread for toasting and a tin of golden syrup.

Eustace sat staring into the fire, half-mesmerised by the leaping flames. He was struggling to make sense of the evening's events. 'Most peculiar,' he said at last. 'The barley water couldn't have been poisoned until after Old Bramble Head entered the room.'

'How do you know that?' asked Master Oliver Davenport.

'Because if the poison was already in the goblet, then the Great Aunt would have been dead *before* Old Bramble Head came in,' said Eustace. 'If only Percival hadn't run off. We really do need to search for him as soon as it's light.'

The door opened and Inspector Hanwell entered sheepishly.

'Hello again, Inspector,' said Eustace, with a sigh of relief. 'What a pleasant surprise.' It was a lie, of course, but even the arrival of the Inspector was infinitely preferable to a visit from Old Bramble Head.

'I'm not happy about this,' said the Inspector. 'I won't say more than that, but I'm not happy, see?' He slowly lowered himself on to the rug and sat beside the fire with his legs crossed. 'Your aunt sent me up here, while the butler sorts me out a room.'

'Would you like some toast?' asked Horatio, pronging two slices of bread on the toasting fork and holding them close to the glowing coals.

'I don't know why they've sent me up here with

you lot,' mumbled the Inspector. 'Honest to goodness I don't.'

'Is it because you're small?' asked Loveday

The Inspector scowled at the girl. 'What I lack in height I more than make up for in brains,' he said.

This seemed unlikely, but the children had been well brought up and knew better than to contradict their elders. They sat in silence and waited for the bread to toast.

'One slice, or two?' asked Horatio, offering the toasting fork to the Inspector.

'Didn't say I was hungry, did I?' snarled the man. 'You're taking a blooming liberty, you are.'

'Well, if you're *not* hungry ...' began Eustace, taking the slices of toast from the fork and dropping them on to his own plate.

'And I didn't say that neither,' said the Inspector hurriedly, snatching the toast from Eustace and proceeding to smear it thickly with golden syrup from the tin. Suddenly, a trickle of blood dribbled from his left nostril. 'I get nosebleeds,' he explained.

'When the cold and the wet gets into my bones.' He tried to staunch the flow of blood with his fingers, but it was a persistent trickle.

'I've got my pocket handkerchief,' said Loveday, tugging a frayed rag from her pocket and holding it out for the Inspector. 'I've only used it once.'

Inspector Hanwell took the handkerchief, twisted a corner tightly and inserted it up his nostril. 'I'll just sit here quiet and wait for it to clot,' he muttered, turning his back on the children and crunching his toast hungrily.

Eustace groaned at the noise. 'Do please chew with your mouth closed.'

'I've got me nose plugged, haven't I?' said the Inspector bitterly. 'If I chewed with me mouth shut I'd most probably suffocate.'

Eustace was about to reply but thought better of it. Matters were already quite serious enough without a third corpse to contend with.

Chapter Ten

A Dread Figure From the Marshes

THE NEXT MORNING the children woke early, intending to search the island for Percival by first light. But light was in short supply, and a treacherous pall of mist shrouded Bleakley Manor.

'He's probably drowned in the marsh by now,' said Loveday grimly. 'Unless he's hiding somewhere inside the house.'

'Can crime-solving wait until after breakfast?' asked Horatio, his stomach rumbling in reply to a gurgle from Master Oliver Davenport. 'I'm no good at brain-thinking without eggs and bacon inside me.'

As soon as the children had settled down to breakfast, they began once more to mull over the events of the previous night.

'So why was your great aunt killed, do you think?' asked Master Oliver Davenport, slicing the top from a boiled egg and sprinkling it liberally with pepper.

'There are two likely explanations,' mused Eustace. 'Either she was murdered because the killer stood to gain something by her death, or else she was killed before she could reveal the identity of the murderer at dinner.'

Loveday, who had constructed an obstacle course on the table for Pineapple Cube, marked out with lumps of sugar, watched in disappointment as her pet turned tail and headed instead for the toast rack.

Horatio frowned and lifted the toast out of Pineapple Cube's reach. 'It puts a chap off his grub having to share the breakfast table with a rat.'

Loveday scowled. 'He doesn't like sharing with you awfully much either,' she replied coldly. 'His table manners are much better than yours. At least Pineapple Cube wipes his mouth after eating.'

'What is the next line of inquiry, Eustace?' asked

Master Oliver Davenport, steering the conversation back to the matter at hand.

Eustace sipped his coffee, deep in thought. 'I think we should go down to the kitchen,' he said. 'The lemon barley water was brought up to the dining room from down there. We need to find out exactly how and when the poison was administered, as they say in the mystery books.'

There were footsteps outside and Loveday hastily picked up Pineapple Cube, dropping him safely back into her pocket with a crumb of toast and marmalade to feed on.

The door opened and Uncle Rufus poked his head inside. He was still wearing his dressing gown and slippers, and seemed relieved to see only the children sitting at the table. 'Ah,' he whispered, as he clapped eyes on the dishes of eggs and bacon, 'that's the stuff to bring a fellow round of a morning!' He picked up a plate and piled it high. 'Funny,' he said, helping himself to a chipolata sausage, 'you'd think a corpse or two might put one off one's breakfast. Seems not to be the case though. I'm hungry as a horse. Hungrier, probably.'

'Those were our thoughts exactly,' said Horatio, mopping up his egg with a slice of toast.

Eustace looked up from his breakfast plate as Inspector Hanwell's voice could be heard from outside the dining room.

'And there's a drip that comes in,' said the Inspector. 'Drip, drip, drip it goes, all night long. I'm getting a sniffle,' he complained.

'Yes, yes, Inspector,' came the fractious reply from Aunt Maude. 'You've made your point quite clearly.'

The Inspector sneezed loudly. 'If it turns into something bronchial, you might have another corpse out there in the ice house,' he muttered.

Aunt Maude entered the room, followed by the Inspector, who shuddered as his eyes alighted on the four children.

'Good morning, Inspector,' beamed Eustace. 'Have you breakfasted?'

Inspector Hanwell snorted. 'Whether I've

breakfasted or whether I haven't breakfasted, is nobody's business but mine,' he said, though he was practically drooling at the mouth as Horatio pronged the last chipolata sausage and dropped it on to his plate.

Horton arrived with a fresh pot of coffee and the Inspector transferred his gaze from Horatio to the butler.

'Would you care for a cup of coffee, sir?'

'Coffee?' said the Inspector. 'I haven't got time to be a-sitting here, sipping coffee when there's vital clues want sniffing out.' With another loud sneeze, he sloped away.

———

As soon as breakfast was finished, the children hurried down to the kitchen in search of Percival, but were dismayed to find that Inspector Hanwell had beaten them downstairs and was busily interrogating Violet.

It clearly pained the Inspector that he was dwarfed by the parlourmaid, so he was standing on an upturned egg crate to give himself more height and authority. Violet was moaning miserably, clutching a teacup in her hands.

'Stop snivelling,' snapped the Inspector. 'Unless you've got something to snivel about?'

'Something like what?' gasped Violet.

'Like your guilt, my girl,' said the Inspector and scribbled a note in his book. 'That's what.'

Violet whimpered and the china cup slipped from her fingers and fell to the floor, shattering on the flagstones.

Eustace coughed politely.

The Inspector turned. 'You again, is it?' he grunted. 'Dogging my every footstep.'

'Yes,' beamed Eustace. 'It's us all right.'

The Inspector scowled back at the boy. 'You get right up my nose, you do.'

'I'm sorry you feel that way,' said Eustace. 'I can assure you most sincerely, Inspector, that all we wish to do is assist you with your investigations.'

Loveday stifled a laugh by digging her fingernails

deep into the palms of her hands.

'Why do you talk funny like that?' asked the Inspector.

'I'm not entirely sure that I know what you mean,' said Eustace, his left eyebrow arched quizzically.

'Like that,' said the Inspector. 'Strange-sounding. Not like a boy at all.'

He turned back to Violet. 'My thinking is this, my girl. Percival gave you the poison to put in the old lady's lemon barley water, and you dribbled it into the decanter when the footman come in disguised as Old Bramble Head. What do you think to that, eh?'

'It's not true,' wailed Violet.

'That's what you say,' replied the Inspector. 'But we've only got your word for that, haven't we?'

'My word's just as good as anyone else's word, ain't it?' moaned Violet. 'I didn't do no poisoning, and nor did Percy … I mean Percival.'

'*Percy*, is it?' crowed the Inspector, clapping his hands together triumphantly. 'Now we start to get to the truth! The footman won your heart over, is that it? And then you carried out the crimes together?'

Wiping her hands on her apron, Cook bustled forward and put a protective arm around Violet's trembling shoulders. 'You're frightening her,' she snapped. 'She's got a delicate nature, that one.'

'Guilty conscience, more like,' said the Inspector.

'You leave poor Violet alone,' said Cook, sternly wagging a finger at the Inspector. 'I'm not as green as I am cabbage-looking. I know what you're trying to do. Trying to scare confessions out of the girl when you ought to know better.'

'None of your business who I'm a-scaring confessions out of,' said the Inspector. 'If I *was* a-scaring confessions. Which I'm not.'

'Well, it *is* my business,' said Cook adamantly. 'What goes on below stairs in my kitchen is very much my business. So, stop upsetting Violet, or else.'

'Or else what?' snorted the Inspector. 'That's what I'd like to know.'

'I can stop cooking you your meals, for a start,' said Cook defiantly, waving her finger again. 'That's what.'

This put a new complexion on matters and the Inspector seemed to crumple. Loveday was tempted to applaud Cook but decided against it.

Muttering at the children as he passed, Inspector Hanwell trudged up the stairs from the kitchen.

'I think the Inspector's rather upset her,' said Horatio quietly, as Violet swept up the pieces of broken crockery.

'She's a good girl,' said Cook. 'She doesn't mean no harm to no one.'

'You mean she's not the poisoning type?' asked Horatio.

'Oh, she could poison people all right,' said Cook, 'but not deliberately. That's why I keep her away from the custard. Lumpy doesn't begin to describe it.'

Violet uttered another loud whimper and ran to hide inside the larder.

Cook rolled her eyes and stoked up the fire in the enormous kitchen range. 'I'm all at sixes and sevens this morning,' she complained. 'Two of them lying dead and cold in the ice house who won't be having so much as another mouthful of food, bless their mortal souls.'

Violet moaned once more from her hideaway.

'You come out of that larder now,' said Cook. 'Don't want you blubbing over my cold game pie. A nerve tonic, that's what you need, my girl. Or a good dose of liver salts. That'll sort you out.'

The children left Cook to console Violet and headed upstairs. As they walked along the hall towards the drawing room, Master Oliver Davenport stopped suddenly and stood stock-still at a window, gazing out across the sweep of rain-soaked lawn towards the marsh.

'What's up?' laughed Loveday. 'You look as though you've seen a ghost!'

'Look!' gasped Master Oliver Davenport. 'Look outside!' The children gathered at the window beside him in time to see a strange figure, half-stumbling across the lawn towards them, covered from head to foot in green marsh slime. 'It's Old Bramble Head!'

The children ran from the hall and out on to the front steps of Bleakley Manor, as the dread figure from the marsh staggered on through the deep grass towards the house, its eyes wild and staring, its long arms flailing desperately.

'That's not Old Bramble Head,' exclaimed Loveday at last. 'It's Percival!'

Violet, who had clearly formed the same conclusion, ran out from the kitchen with Horton close at her heels. 'Percy!' she shrieked. 'We thought you was done for!'

'Better for you if you had drowned in the marshes,' said Horton grimly. 'Sir Max and Lady Bleakley welcomed you in and gave you their trust. And how do you repay them? By bringing shame on this house.'

Percival hung his head, clearly stricken by the accusation. 'Round and round by the edge of the marsh I walked,' he murmured. 'I didn't know where I was going. I was half-mad with terror!'

'It's all right, Percy,' whispered Violet, pulling the

worst of the pond slime from the footman's hair and attempting to dry his sodden clothes by rubbing hard with a towel she had brought with her from the kitchen. 'You're safe now.'

'Shows what you know, my girl,' said a voice, and Violet turned to see Inspector Hanwell approaching across the drive. 'I thought as much,' he continued. 'The footman and the maid acting in league together.'

'Violet didn't have nothing to do with nothing!' cried Percival.

'Ah!' said the Inspector triumphantly. 'So you're not denying *you're* to blame then?'

'No,' stammered Percival. 'What I meant to say ... what I meant to say was ...'

'Well,' said the Inspector, rubbing his hands together for effect, 'I think we'd better go up and search your room now, hadn't we? High time we got to the bottom of things.'

The children followed Inspector Hanwell and Percival inside and up the stairs to the servants' quarters.

'But haven't you already searched his room?' asked Eustace.

'Didn't have the key before, did I?' said the Inspector glumly. 'And your aunt wouldn't let me batter the door down.' He turned to Percival. 'Now, where is it?'

Percival sighed and lifted a loose board in the floor. He reached down and retrieved a key, which he turned in the lock.

The Inspector pushed the man aside and slowly turned the door handle, as though he was half-expecting an accomplice to spring out from behind. The room was a shambolic mess and had an unmistakable smell of carbolic soap and boot polish.

'He's even more untidy than you, Horatio,' whispered Eustace, and was rewarded with a punch on the arm.

'What's this then?' said the Inspector, pulling back a blanket to reveal the grinning sackcloth face of Old Bramble Head.

Eustace jerked back in surprise, hitting his head

on the coat hook behind him.

'That's nothing to do with me,' gulped Percival. 'Someone's been up here and planted that!'

'More and more incriminating all the time,' said the Inspector. He opened a small chest of drawers in a dark corner of the room and rummaged through the footman's clothes. Reaching deep, he lifted out a silver muffin dish and a large silver fish slice. 'Quite the little haul we've got here.'

'It wasn't me that put them there,' gasped Percival. 'And I didn't do nothing with that awful great grinning head!'

'A likely story,' growled the Inspector. 'Now what've we got here then?' he said, lifting out a small bottle that had been concealed inside a sock at the very bottom of the drawer. He unscrewed the lid and sniffed at the contents. 'Know what that is, do you?'

Percival shook his head blankly.

'Of course you do,' said the Inspector. 'Cyanide. The very same that you slipped into the old lady's lemon barley water.' He turned triumphantly to

Aunt Maude who had just arrived outside the door. 'This is what happens when you invite the criminal element into your home,' he said. 'Always check references, when it comes to servants, that's what I say. Always check references.'

'His references were impeccable,' said Aunt Maude defensively.

'Forged, I daresay,' said the Inspector.

'But it doesn't make any sense,' whispered Eustace to Loveday. 'Why didn't he take the silver with him when he fled the house?'

Loveday nodded. 'And why on earth did he come back?'

'What's going to happen to Percival now?' Eustace asked the Inspector.

'He's going to be arrested,' the Inspector replied, pulling out a pair of handcuffs from the pocket of his overcoat. 'That's what's going to happen to him.' He fastened the cuffs around Percival's trembling wrists. 'It'll be the noose for you, m'lad. That's something to be mulling over now, isn't it?'

When the Inspector was satisfied that Percival could not escape through the window without falling to his certain death, he locked the door and pocketed the key. 'He won't be getting out now, not for love nor money.'

The children followed Inspector Hanwell downstairs to the dining room.

'Well, I've solved the murders!' said the Inspector, grinning broadly. 'So what do you think of that? All about as neat and tidy as can be.'

Eustace opened and closed his mouth but not a sound came out.

'Lost for words, eh?' said the Inspector, ringing the servants' bell beside the fireplace.

And it was true – Eustace was indeed lost for words.

Horton appeared from the hall. 'You rang, sir?'

'I did, my good man,' said the Inspector grandly. 'Tell Cook I'll have cutlets for my luncheon. And gravy. Plenty of gravy. And I wouldn't say no to a spoonful of that mustard piccalilli the family seems so partial to. I'm quite fond of a dollop of mustard piccalilli. Then a nice suet pudding for my afters.' He grinned again at the children. 'Now leave me be,' he said, rubbing his hands together. 'I've worked up quite an appetite. Crime-solving is hungry work!'

Chapter Eleven

An Imposter is Unmasked

THE CHILDREN LEFT Inspector Hanwell smugly anticipating the arrival of grilled cutlets and gravy.

'Buck up, old chap,' said Horatio to his brother. 'Better luck next time.'

Eustace shook his head defiantly. 'I'm not giving up yet,' he said. It seemed incredible to the boy that they had been outfoxed by the Inspector. Yet all the evidence seemed to point to one conclusion: that the footman was indeed the guilty party. 'I think we should go up and speak to Percival ourselves. There's something about this mystery that seems too neat and tidy.'

'Who is it?' came Percival's muffled voice from behind his bedroom door. 'Violet, is that you?'

The children stood outside, with a slice of buttered toast that they had brought up from the kitchen.

'It's Eustace Bleakley,' whispered the boy.

'And the rest of us,' added Loveday, breaking off a corner of the toast to feed to Pineapple Cube.

Eustace peered through the keyhole and could make out the figure of the footman sitting miserably on his bed with the curtains drawn. 'We'd like to ask you some questions.'

There came a disgruntled sniff from the other side of the door. 'I'll tell you the very same thing I told that inspector,' said Percival. 'I didn't kill nobody and I didn't scarper with no silverware. I've been set up, that's what's happened.'

'Very well,' said Eustace. 'But why did you go to all the trouble of disguising yourself as Old Bramble Head at dinner last night?'

'That weren't me and that's the honest truth of the matter,' groaned Percival. 'I wasn't even in the house.' He stopped. 'I'm not saying another word more.'

'We've brought you something to eat,' said Loveday, suddenly remembering the slice of toast and sliding it under the door.

'Toast?' said Percival in surprise.

'If it was anything larger, we wouldn't have been able to post it through to you,' said Loveday. 'It might be rather dusty though.'

'Every man has to have his peck of dirt,' said Percival sadly. 'Isn't that what they say?'

Loveday pushed Eustace aside and watched through the keyhole as Percival, still handcuffed, picked up the toast and took a bite.

'You're not bad kids,' he said, 'I'll say that much. For all your meddling ways.'

'I'm hoping that our meddling might be the very thing that keeps you from the hangman's noose,' whispered Eustace.

'Go on,' said Percival, with grim curiosity. 'I'm listening.'

'Why did you run away from the house?' began Eustace. 'That was a foolish thing to do. It looked like an admission of guilt.'

Percival sniffed hard. 'I know that well enough,' he grunted between mouthfuls of toast. 'But when you've been locked away in prison like what I was, nobody takes your word for it when you says how you haven't done this, or you haven't done that. I knew it was hopeless, but I fled all the same.'

'How did you come to be in prison in the first place?' asked Loveday.

'I was in service to Lord Crutchley,' replied Percival. 'I worked as Under Footman there for two years. Hard as flint, he was. And I stole from him, as you know, to serve him right for the way he'd treated me.'

'That's no excuse for stealing,' said Master Oliver Davenport. 'No matter how much of an old miser he was.'

'I'm not saying it was right, 'cause it wasn't,' said Percival, a pained note in his voice. 'But I did my time in prison, sewing mail bags and this and that. And locked away in my cell, with only the earwigs and the beetles for company, I said to myself, "Percy," I said, "You've turned your back on a life of crime and that's an end to it."'

'Very commendable,' said Eustace encouragingly. 'And how did you come to hear that there was a position at Bleakley Manor?'

'An employment agency wrote to me special,' answered Percival. 'Sent me a letter, they did, the day after I got out of prison. Asked me if I was looking to go back into service again. Only I didn't have no references to speak of, just a letter from the Prison Governor to say I'd put my burgling ways behind me. So I wrote to the agency and told them as much. And to let them know I wasn't afraid of hard work,' he added defensively.

'Of course not,' said Eustace, eager to reassure the penitent footman.

'What happened then?' asked Horatio.

'They wrote and said that I wasn't to worry that I

had no references as that would all be taken care of,' said Percival.

'Fortunate indeed,' said Eustace.

'I couldn't hardly believe my luck,' continued Percival. 'It was like all my birthdays and Christmases had come at once.'

Eustace clicked his tongue, lost in thought.

'Did you speak to anyone at the agency in person?' asked Horatio. 'On the telephone or—'

'No, Master Horatio,' interrupted Percival, 'they only communicated by letter.'

'And you didn't think that was slightly fishy?' asked Loveday.

'No, miss,' murmured Percival, his voice faltering. He stopped and let out a deep breath. 'That's to say, it did seem a *bit* irregular, only when you've served time behind bars it's hard to get employment in a house of quality like this is, so you takes your chances.'

'Do you still have the letter?' asked Horatio.

'In my chest of drawers, I think,' replied Percival.

'And may we see it?' whispered Eustace urgently.

There was a pause as Percival searched through the chest, his handcuffs rattling. At last a small envelope emerged from beneath the door.

Eustace opened the envelope and pulled out a folded sheet of writing paper embossed in red with the letters:

B.A.D.I.

'B.A.D.I.,' whispered Eustace through the keyhole. 'Do you know what the initials stand for?'

'I don't,' said Percival.

'Tell us,' said Loveday, who could remain patient no longer, 'why exactly *did* you run away last night?'

'I overheard Mr Horton talking to Cook,' said Percival with a sorrowful sigh. 'He told her he suspected me of pinching silverware from his pantry. I knew the Inspector would pin the Colonel's murder on me the moment he heard about my stretch in prison, so I fled the house before dinner was served. I wouldn't never have come back neither, if it wasn't for the marsh and the broken bridge.'

'May we keep the letter from the employment agency?' asked Eustace. 'I think it might turn out to be a very significant clue.'

Percival let out a hopeless sigh. 'Be my guest,' he said. 'But if that's all the evidence that's keeping me from the noose, then I don't much fancy my chances.'

'Do you think Percival was telling the truth?' asked Master Oliver Davenport. 'About not having dressed up as Old Bramble Head at the Michaelmas celebrations?'

'I do,' said Eustace. 'Although I can't for the life of me think who else it could have been.'

'Maybe it really *was* Old Bramble Head after all?' said Master Oliver Davenport, with a half-hearted laugh.

They were passing the door to Great Aunt Henrietta's room when Eustace stopped. If the Inspector was so certain that he had apprehended his culprit, Eustace would make the most of his new freedom to investigate. He turned the handle and opened the door.

The room was exactly as the Great Aunt had left it, before descending the staircase for her fateful last dinner. The Devonshire cream had yellowed in the bowl and a bluebottle hovered above, circling drunkenly.

'You don't think the Great Aunt got carried away and accidentally poisoned herself?' suggested Horatio.

'She was a writer,' said Loveday. 'As a writer myself, I understand the creative temperament. The old pill was eccentric, but she wasn't batty.'

Eustace leaned over the desk, peering closely at the indentations in Great Aunt Henrietta's blotter.

'It looks as though she'd just written someone a note,' he said, excitedly. Taking his pencil from his pocket, he rubbed gently over the blotter paper until the Great Aunt's words were revealed:

Reverend 'Saline-Crum',
I see you have changed your name since we met at
the Tippitburr Mission in India — but a leopard
cannot change his spots.

Though Eustace strained his eyes, he could make out no more; the writing on the blotter became too faint and indistinct to read.

'The plot thickens!' he said, tapping his pencil against the paper. 'The Reverend said he'd never met Great Aunt Henrietta. I think we've caught him out in a lie!'

'We'd better go and find the bounder then,' said Loveday with a grim and determined expression. 'I'll fetch my lacrosse stick. There are dark deeds afoot and weaponry may be called for!'

The children found the Reverend Saline-Crum standing alone in the library, hymn book in hand, staring gloomily from the window.

He turned his head as the children entered the room and his eyes opened wider than ever.

Without uttering a word, Loveday held up the sheet of paper from the Great Aunt's blotter.

'Oh,' said the Reverend brokenly, 'then you know, do you?'

Loveday nodded.

Defeated, the Reverend sank into an armchair and clutched a cushion to his chest.

'When we saw the note we knew you and the Great Aunt had met before,' said Eustace smoothly, 'even though you claimed that you'd never laid eyes on her before you came to Bleakley Manor.'

'So Saline-Crum isn't your real name?' said Master Oliver Davenport.

The Reverend shook his head sadly. 'It is an alias, I am afraid. My family were in the biscuit manufacturing trade. They made salt biscuits for the navy. "Saline-Crum" struck me as a suitable alternative to Arthurton. My real name, you understand.'

'But why pretend you're someone else?' asked Master Oliver Davenport.

The Reverend took a deep breath. 'I have a love,' he confided.

'Romance, you mean?' said Loveday. 'An unrequited passion for the Great Aunt?'

'Oh no,' said the Reverend, colouring around the cheeks and casting his eyes towards the fireplace. 'A love of *taxidermy*. Stuffed animals of infinite variety. And when I like a piece, I'm afraid that I will stop at nothing until I have acquired it. I am particularly fond of hamsters in waistcoats.'

'Hamsters?' said Loveday. 'Like those awful things upstairs in the Family Museum?'

'Oh yes,' said the Reverend in awe. '*A Night at the Opera*. A most exceptional piece!'

'Exceptionally ugly,' replied Loveday.

'But you *do* think that hamsters are adorable, do you not?' said the Reverend with a far-off look in his eye. 'Surely you must? The charming smiles on their furry faces. The appealing way they stare at one through their little glass eyes. Can any animal wear a waistcoat quite so well as a hamster? I think not.'

'I like hamsters well enough when they're alive,' said Loveday with a scowl. 'But not when they're dead and stuffed.'

The Reverend gave a spluttering laugh of surprise.

'If they weren't dead, how on earth would it be possible to dress them in waistcoats?' he asked. 'They would never keep still for long enough!'

'I still don't understand why you changed your name, or what hold the Great Aunt had over you,' said Horatio impatiently. 'What business of hers was it if you liked hamsters in waistcoats or if you didn't like hamsters in waistcoats?'

The Reverend gazed miserably at his inquisitor. 'Then I will relate the sorry saga,' he said. 'There was one piece in particular that I had always coveted: a tableau of the Battle of Lochburney, played out with hamsters in the uniforms of the English and Scots soldiers. Ah ... the most *exquisite* tartan kilts for the Scots hamsters.' He closed his eyes and wrung his hands together, overwhelmed by the mere recollection of the object. 'It was a most wonderful example of the taxidermist's art. A great rarity.' A mist of perspiration had formed on the Reverend's forehead and he dabbed at his face with a pocket handkerchief. 'The tableau was in the private collection of the Maharaja of Tippitburr, who was a great connoisseur of hamsters in costume … and to a lesser extent, guinea pigs.'

'I wanted a guinea pig,' interjected Master Oliver Davenport. 'But we aren't allowed them at school.'

The Reverend Saline-Crum bit his lower lip and nodded. 'Oh no, quite right,' he said. 'It is my humble opinion that guinea pigs were not set upon this earth to be dressed in clothes. They lack the sartorial majesty of the hamster.'

'The what, please?' asked Master Oliver Davenport.

'I mean to say,' explained the Reverend, 'they are ill-suited for trousers. Give me a hamster any day of the week … and stuff it.'

'Back to the sorry saga though,' said Loveday, before the conversation could stray any further, 'did you pinch the tableau from Maharaja what's-his-name or not?'

'Well, no,' said the Reverend, 'but when, on the Maharaja's death, I discovered that the piece was to be auctioned …' He coughed nervously into his handkerchief. 'The tale does not reflect well on me, I confess. I bid beyond my means. I suppose you might say I robbed Peter to pay Paul.'

Loveday raised her eyebrows. 'You mean you stole the money to buy it?'

'Borrowed,' said the Reverend, adding in a barely audible whisper, 'from missionary funds.'

'I see,' said Eustace, clasping his hands behind his back, as detectives often do in crime stories.

The Reverend let out a low moan. 'It had been my intention to pay back the sum, of course,' he said. 'But missionaries are not well paid. And alas, your Great Aunt, who was on a visit to Tippitburr to research a book, discovered me in the act of … of …'

'Pilfering?' suggested Loveday helpfully, and the Reverend nodded, his eyelids drooping heavily as though the strain of keeping them open had finally defeated him.

'I returned to England at once and changed my name, in case your Great Aunt told anyone what she had discovered about me.'

'So, you came to Bleakley Manor to do in the late Great Aunt, did you?' said Horatio. 'Because she knew too much? And I suppose the Colonel got wind of it and you did him in too?'

'Oh, no,' said the Reverend, his eyes wide in horror. 'I will admit it was an almighty blow to find your Great Aunt here – I knew at once that she would expose me – but I wished her no harm, and accepted my fate. As for the Colonel, we barely exchanged two words before his unfortunate murder.'

'Then why did you come to Bleakley Manor in the first place?' asked Eustace.

'To examine your uncle's collection of taxidermy, of course,' said the Reverend, brightening again for a moment. '*A Night at the Opera* – a very fine tableau indeed!'

'What are you going to do now?' asked Loveday, her hand reaching towards the lacrosse stick. 'Will you come clean and admit that you stole the money? Or will we have to resort to harsher measures?'

Eustace shot Loveday a sharp glance and she withdrew her hand, leaving the lacrosse stick where it was.

'Like a husk, tossed on the winds of ill fortune,' said the Reverend Saline-Crum at last, rising slowly from his armchair. 'My path seems clear to me now. As soon as the bridge is repaired and we can leave the island, I shall waste no time in speaking to the Bishop. I will throw myself on his tender mercies. You need not fear that I will attempt to abscond without making amends for my actions.' He bowed his head and took his leave.

'Do you believe him?' asked Horatio as soon as he was certain that the Reverend had passed out of earshot.

'I don't,' said Loveday. 'He hasn't the slightest intention of confessing to the Bish. I've seen the type. The Reverend Saline-Crum will be pilfering the loose change from the collection plate by next evensong.'

'But murder?' asked Master Oliver Davenport.

'He had motive and opportunity,' said Horatio. 'He was sitting beside Great Aunt Henrietta at dinner – he could easily have poisoned her lemon barley water. But does he have the stomach for murder?'

Eustace was not so sure. 'I don't believe so. And why kill the Colonel? It hardly seems likely that Great Aunt Henrietta let on to him about the Reverend's murky past.'

'Then we're no further on than when we started,' sighed Loveday.

'I'm afraid not,' said Eustace.

'Maybe Percy really is guilty?' said Master Oliver Davenport.

'Let's go and talk to Violet,' decided Eustace. 'Perhaps she might be able to cast some light on this mystery.'

Chapter Twelve

The Plot Thickens

THE CHILDREN FOUND Violet in the dining room, weeping as she polished the wooden floor with a tin of Eazee-Wax polish.

'Whatever's the matter, Violet?' asked Loveday, hurrying into the room.

'Nothing, miss,' said Violet, 'it's just the awful things that's been happening, it's set my nerves on edge. First the Colonel, and now the old lady with her lemon barley water.' She polished away a pool of tears with the floor cloth. 'I wish to goodness I never—' She stopped suddenly and her mouth gaped open.

'You wish you'd never what?' asked Eustace. 'Tell us what you know, Violet.'

'It was me what took up the lemon barley water,' said Violet, her face white with fear. 'But I didn't pour in no poison,' she moaned. 'I've never thought no ill of no one. I haven't, honest.' She attempted to polish the floor again but her tears were falling more quickly than she could mop them up.

'We believe you,' said Loveday, convinced that Violet was incapable of murdering two people in cold blood without drowning the house in tears. 'You don't have to convince us.'

'Oh, miss, you are kind, miss,' said Violet with a sniff. 'Bless you. But it's no good, miss, they'll more than likely send me to the block to have my poor old head lopped off.'

'They don't use beheading now,' said Horatio, 'they'd most probably hang you by the neck until you're—'

Eustace hastily interrupted. 'But you're not a suspect, Violet,' he assured her, 'at least, not as far as we're concerned.'

Violet let out a deep breath. 'The Inspector still

thinks it's Percival what done it, don't he?' she said. 'He hasn't changed his mind about that, has he?'

'I'm afraid he hasn't,' said Eustace.

'He's awful handsome,' said Violet with a trembling lower lip that threatened to break into a smile. 'Percy, I mean. Not the Inspector. *He's* more like some old toad.'

'Yes, *that's* what he looks like,' agreed Loveday with a snort of laughter. 'I've been racking my brains trying to think what it is he reminds me of.'

'But Percy's like someone out the movies, ain't he?' continued Violet, warming to her theme. 'Those eyes he's got. Have you seen his eyes?'

Loveday replied that she had indeed noticed that Percival had eyes.

'I'm no beauty to look at, not like them stars in 'Ollywood,' said Violet, raising her head and smiling to reveal a set of grey and crooked teeth, 'but me 'eart's in the right place. And that's what Percy likes about me.' She whimpered again and wiped her nose on her sleeve. 'He don't mean no harm, miss,' she whispered. 'You see, he told it all to me, he did. Right from the start. Me and me alone. That he come from prison for pinchin' silver from his last employer what was a wicked ol' skinflint what deserved to 'ave the very shirt stole from off 'is back.'

'He must have told Horton as well,' said Loveday. 'About his prison record. Because Horton told our aunt and uncle.'

'I don't know about that,' said Violet uncertainly. 'All I do know is that when Percy got let out, he mended his ways – I *know* he did. But who's going to listen to a man what's seen time behind bars, that's what Percy says. They'll more than likely string 'im up and blame the 'ole wretched lot on him.' Her lip quivered and she began to weep again.

The children did their best to cheer Violet's spirits, but it seemed that she was happiest when left alone with her sorrows. So they left her alone with her sorrows.

As they wandered along the hallway, the children encountered Horton, who nodded his head to them as he passed by carrying a tray of food.

'Creamed oysters on toast,' whispered Eustace, 'most probably for Uncle Rufus. If we scoot downstairs quickly we can search through Horton's pantry before he returns.'

'What are we looking for?' asked Horatio.

'Violet said she was the only one that Percival told about his criminal past,' said Eustace. 'So I want to know how Horton knew.'

Cook was busy peeling potatoes at the kitchen table, so the children were able to tiptoe past to the butler's pantry while her back was turned. Silently they slipped inside and pushed the door closed behind them.

Eustace sat in the chair and opened the drawers of the desk, but could find no letter outlining Percival's criminal past, only an old book with a scuffed leather cover.

'*Buried Treasures of Ancient Egypt*,' he read in surprise. 'Horton must have hidden depths.'

He passed the book to his brother, who was

leaning against the great metal door of the Airtight Silver Safe. Horatio flicked through the book disinterestedly.

'Hello, what's this?' said Horatio, removing a sheet of paper that had been trapped between the pages.

THE STOAT AND RAVEN
LUDD-ON-LYE
FENSHIRE

<u>One night's room and board.</u>
10 shillings and sixpence.
PAID BY B.A.D.I.

'Look at this,' said Horatio. 'The initials B.A.D.I. again. Whatever can they stand for?'

Eustace took Percival's letter from his pocket. 'Haven't the foggiest,' he replied. 'The B might stand for "bureau", I suppose? And perhaps D for "domestic servants"?'

At the sound of approaching footsteps, Eustace

turned suddenly and the bill slipped from his fingers. As he stooped to retrieve the sheet of paper, it was lifted by a sudden draught from beneath the door of the silver safe.

'Horton's coming back,' hissed Loveday. 'We'll have to scarper by the back steps, we can't risk going through the kitchen. Quickly!'

———

The children huddled for warmth beside the fire in the old nursery. They had been so engrossed in their investigations that when they had finally burst into the dining room for lunch, the dishes had long since been cleared away. Flames leapt cheerfully in the grate as Master Oliver Davenport arranged the necessary paraphernalia for tea and Loveday busily and hungrily buttered toast.

'I know the solution's there, if only I could see it,' said Eustace. 'It really is the most devilish of mysteries.'

'You can have Pineapple Cube for half an hour, if you want?' said Loveday, gently lifting the rat from her pocket. 'Whenever I can't think things through properly, Pineapple Cube sort of shows me the way.'

The rat hissed, its whiskers twitching wildly. 'I shall manage, thank you,' said Eustace.

Horatio closed his eyes, conscious of a dull ache in the middle of his forehead, the result of over-thinking. 'If it *wasn't* Percival, then who could it possibly have been?' he groaned. 'Certainly not another Bleakley or one of the guests; they were all in the dining room with us.'

'We know it can't be Horton,' said Loveday, 'because he was locked in the silver safe. And he couldn't have been in two places at once, could he?'

Though Horatio had only a shaky grasp of physics, even he was certain the man could not. 'And Cook had been drugged,' he said. 'Unless she was only *pretending* to be drugged, of course?'

'She did say she was tempted to kill sometimes …' said Loveday. 'She was rather mysterious on that score.'

Master Oliver Davenport nodded. 'And she was

awfully cross with your Great Aunt for criticising her mayonnaise.'

'I believe Cook,' said Eustace, neatly cutting his toast into triangles and spreading them thickly with blackcurrant jam. 'But even if I didn't, whoever it was inside that costume was much taller than her.'

'Shall I be mother?' asked Master Oliver Davenport, holding up the teapot.

'Pour away,' said Eustace. 'But not too much milk. I need a strong cup of tea to stimulate my brain cells. And five sugars. No, seven. My brain will thank you for it.'

Master Oliver Davenport poured the tea. 'So it must have been Percival then,' he concluded. 'Unless it really *was* Old Bramble Head in the flesh.'

Eustace sipped his tea slowly. 'The more everyone says it must be Percival,' he said, 'the more I'm absolutely convinced that it isn't.'

Horatio stood up and peered out through the window. Though a thick mist was fast settling over the garden, he could still dimly make out the brick dome of the ice house. 'It's rather odd,' he said, 'to think we're only a stone's throw from two half-frozen corpses.'

'Has everything got to be corpses?' asked Master Oliver Davenport. 'Not that I don't find corpses fascinating, of course,' he added hurriedly, fearing that he might be left out of the investigations if he complained too bitterly, 'but maybe we can have a little rest from murderings until we've polished off our grub?'

Eustace nodded and smiled at the boy, and the children sat and ate in silence until every last slice of buttered toast had been eaten.

'I'm perfectly happy to talk about corpses now,' grinned Master Oliver Davenport at last, wiping butter from his mouth on the sleeve of his pullover. 'It's only when I'm eating.'

'What's this?' said Eustace, picking up his pocket notebook and pointing at a buttery stain on the list of suspects.

'Sorry,' said Master Oliver Davenport hanging

his head. 'That was me.'

Eustace tutted. 'It doesn't make us look very professional if we hand in our findings smeared in butter.'

'The Inspector got syrup on some of *his* evidence,' said Master Oliver Davenport defensively.

'That's precisely what I mean,' said Eustace. '*Not* very professional.' He climbed to his feet and brushed the toast crumbs from his pullover. 'It's all so infuriating. Like a jigsaw with a missing piece. I think we should go back to the beginning and examine Uncle Max's study again, but this time without the Inspector getting in our way.'

———

Aunt Maude, Uncle Rufus and the Reverend Saline-Crum were engaged in a game of bridge in the drawing room, and the children were able to tiptoe past the open door and into Sir Max's study without being seen. The room was in darkness, so they switched on the desk lamp and closed the door.

Loveday, who had brought Pineapple Cube with

her from the old nursery, lowered the rat on to the rug and allowed it to roam freely.

'I don't know what you expect us to find that we haven't found already,' said Horatio, gazing blankly around the room.

Eustace shook his head hopelessly. 'I don't know either,' he groaned, hoping that inspiration would strike like a bolt from the blue.

Loveday had dropped to the floor and was crawling across the rug in hot pursuit of Pineapple Cube. 'What have you got there?' she purred. 'Have you found something to eat?' The rat was busily gnawing at the corner of a wooden panel in the wall.

'Just like Mustard!' said Horatio, remembering the wolfhound's strange behaviour the previous morning. 'I think he must have worked the wood loose from the wall.' He pressed hard at the panel, and with a creak of ancient hinges it swung towards him.

The children gasped as they found themselves staring into a dark hole that had opened up in the wall. Pineapple Cube was preparing to scuttle through, when Loveday scooped him up and dropped him back into her pocket.

'A secret passage!' exclaimed Master Oliver Davenport, with all the wonder of an archaeologist who had stumbled upon an unopened tomb.

Horatio took a box of matches from the mantelpiece. Striking a match, he reached inside the hole and peered into the dark space beyond. He could just make out the faintest glimmer of a light in the distance. The passageway was no more than twelve feet long and four feet wide, with a low ceiling.

Unable to contain his curiosity, Horatio climbed through the hole and into the tunnel.

'Be careful,' hissed Eustace. 'The ceiling might not be safe.'

'It's probably been here for hundreds of years,' said Horatio, disappearing into the darkness. 'I expect it will stay up for another five minutes.'

One by one, the children followed Horatio through the hole. They soon found themselves climbing down a set of rough stone steps, until they arrived at the end of the passage, where their way was barred by another wooden panel. Horatio pressed his eye against a knothole.

'Can you see anything?' whispered Master Oliver Davenport.

Horatio, who had read more adventure stories than Latin or algebra books, was expecting to see a hidden treasure hoard or a torturer's dungeon. He was not at all prepared for the sight that he beheld.

'It's a little kitchen,' he gasped.

Edging his way past Loveday, Eustace moved Horatio aside so he too could look through the hole.

'It's a bit of squeeze in here,' said Master Oliver Davenport, who found himself squashed between Loveday and Horatio.

'Watch what you're doing!' hissed Loveday, as the boy wriggled to get comfortable.

Pineapple Cube squeaked indignantly and Master Oliver Davenport yelped in pain. 'He's got me!' said the boy, as the rat poked his head out of Loveday's pocket and bit him viciously on the finger. He shook his hand desperately to free it from Pineapple Cube's pin-sharp teeth and caught Horatio a glancing blow on the side of the head. Stumbling backwards, Horatio fell hard against his brother, propelling him through the wooden panel and into the tiny kitchen beyond. Horatio, Master Oliver Davenport and Loveday tumbled out after him.

'It's Uncle Max's secret pickling laboratory!' said Eustace, picking himself up off the floor and brushing down his trousers. 'So he was telling the truth after all!' It was a narrow room lit by electric light, with a high ceiling and a plaster frieze running around the walls, decorated with each and every variety of vegetable that Sir Max had ever pickled. In the corner was a small stove and sink, and all about hung the overpowering aroma of boiled vinegar. 'This must be where he slips away to do his secret pickling,' continued Eustace. It means he can be boiling up pickles in here when Aunt Maude thinks he's safely tucked away in his study, out of harm's way.'

'This is all very interesting,' said Master Oliver Davenport, who had been patiently sucking his finger. 'But I've just been bitten by a rat and unless I get a sticking plaster soon I think I might very well bleed to death.'

'Come and look at this,' said Horatio, who had discovered another secret door in the panelling on the other side of the room. 'There's another tunnel here,' he said, pushing the door open and peering into the stone chamber beyond. 'I wonder where this one leads.'

Loveday frowned and shook her head. 'Secret passages are all well and good,' she said, 'precisely the sort of place a bounding Yorkshire ferret might lurk in *Murder and Mayhem Magazine*. But I don't see how this helps to solve our mystery. If the Colonel *had* discovered that Sir Max was up to a bit of secret pickling, it was hardly worth murdering him for it, was it? And anyway, when it comes to Great Aunt Henrietta's murder, Sir Max has an airtight alibi.'

'Airtight ...' said Eustace suddenly, and sucked on his lower lip. *'Airtight!'*

'What's up?' asked Horatio.

'Quiet, old thing ...' said Eustace. 'I'm thinking.' Suddenly, his expression brightened. 'I've been an absolute ass!' he cried as he bolted from the pickling laboratory and back along the secret passageway.

Master Oliver Davenport was baffled. 'Don't you want to see where this other passageway leads?'

'I already know!' shouted Eustace, as he disappeared up the stairs.

'Care to let the rest of us in on the secret?' called Horatio, giving chase as one by one they all scrambled after the boy and re-emerged in Sir Max's study.

'The pieces have finally dropped into place!' shouted Eustace, skidding across the polished floor as he made for the door.

Catching up, Horatio put out a hand to stop his brother. 'You're not shamming?' he panted. 'You really do know something?'

'Not something,' replied Eustace, turning with a grin to face Horatio as he opened the study door. 'I know *everything*!'

Chapter Thirteen

A Disappearance and an Arrival

AS SOON AS EUSTACE had explained his solution, the children instructed the surviving members of the Bleakley family – Aunt Maude and Sir Max– in company with Uncle Rufus and the Reverend Saline-Crum, to gather in the drawing room. Cook and Violet had been summoned from the kitchen and stood anxiously beside the fireplace as Horton served coffee.

Inspector Hanwell stood proudly over Percival, his prisoner, who was sitting handcuffed and miserable, throwing the occasional longing glance to Violet.

'We should have left him under lock and key, by rights,' muttered the Inspector to Sir Max. 'Safest place for him. It's not good common sense having the wretch sitting here among us non-murderous folk. If the bridge wasn't down, I'd have carted him off by now.' He grunted in Eustace's direction. 'Well then? If you've got something to say then you might as well say it.'

Eustace cleared his throat.

'Are you ill?' inquired Aunt Maude. 'You know I object to germs.'

'No, Aunt,' replied Eustace. 'I was collecting my thoughts.'

'Well, collect them quicker then,' said the Inspector. 'Before this 'ere felonious footman tries to make another run for it.'

'I'm not going nowhere,' said Percival miserably. 'I'm innocent and that's that.'

Aunt Maude glared at the man and turned to Inspector Hanwell. 'It's always the silver,' she said, with a sorry shake of her head that set her pearls rattling. 'Once a thief, for evermore a thief.'

'It's not the silver, Aunt Maude,' said Eustace

calmly. 'Percival is entirely blameless in all this.'

'But nobody else has been murdered have they, smart alec?' said the Inspector sneeringly. 'Not since I've had him locked up. If I hadn't apprehended the right man there would have been a third or a fourth murder, most likely. But there hasn't been. So there.'

Eustace waited patiently until the Inspector had run out of steam, then began again. 'It was a very cleverly thought out crime,' he said. 'We were led to believe that it was Uncle Max who was the intended first victim, and not Colonel Theodore.'

'Because more people wanted to do in Uncle Max than Colonel Theodore,' interrupted Loveday.

'I do wish you wouldn't use expressions like "do in",' said Aunt Maude. 'It's a terribly vulgar way of speaking.'

'Anyway,' continued Loveday, 'Uncle Rufus wanted his pots of cash, Aunt Maude hates it when he goes on and on about pickles … and Great Aunt Henrietta didn't like him awfully much, I expect.'

'It's true,' admitted Sir Max. 'She didn't.'

Uncle Rufus stroked his moustache. 'So, you're saying it wasn't a mistake that Theodore was bashed over the noggin with the stuffed crow?'

'That's precisely what we're saying,' said Eustace.

The Inspector sniffed and wiped his nose. 'So what reason was there for doing in –' he glanced at Aunt Maude – 'sorry, m'ladyship, what reason was there for *killing* the Colonel? Somebody wanted to get their hands on his musical nose-thingummy-jig?' He snorted with laughter. 'Is that it?'

'Not that,' said Eustace. 'I would hazard a guess that the murderer was in search of the treasure of Arn Akh.'

'I told Eustace all about that,' said Master Oliver Davenport proudly, waving his copy of *The Archaeological Gazette* for all to see. 'It was rumoured to be hidden inside a terracotta bust from ancient Egypt. The Colonel said he hadn't found it … but the terracotta dust on the floor of his room, and the fact that he was murdered … well, it suggests otherwise, doesn't it?'

'But who else would have known about the treasure?' asked Aunt Maude.

'I know for a fact,' said Eustace, 'that Master Oliver Davenport is not the only person under this roof who has an interest in ancient Egypt.'

Eustace allowed the information to sink in for a moment, then cleared his throat again. 'These are the events as we know them. On Michaelmas Eve, the murderer sent this note to Colonel Theodore, pretending to be Uncle Max,' he continued, holding up the piece of paper. 'He asked the Colonel to meet him in his study at ten o'clock that night. When the Colonel arrived, the murderer was in hiding and hit him over the head with the stuffed crow.'

The Reverend Saline-Crum had been sitting silently, sipping his coffee as he followed the story. 'Excuse me for asking,' he said. 'But am I correct in thinking that the two murders were perpetrated by the same individual?'

This was not quite the order in which Eustace had intended the tale to unfold. 'Yes, you are quite correct, Reverend,' he said. 'But please, one murder at a time.'

'It's just … and excuse me for saying so,' the Reverend continued, 'if the same person carried out both murders, and at the time of the second murder everyone is accounted for *except* Percival, then doesn't it *have* to be him?'

'At last!' grinned the Inspector. 'Someone in this blessed place with an ounce of common sense.'

Eustace shook his head. 'I'm afraid the Reverend isn't quite correct. Not everyone *was* accounted for. Not really.'

The Inspector, who had been smiling smugly at the Reverend's summing up, now looked as though he was about to explode with rage. 'Now, look here,' he shouted, 'we've got our culprit!'

'No, you haven't,' said Loveday. 'But an awful lot of work has gone into making you *think* you have.'

Eustace unfolded the letter from the B.A.D.I. employment agency.

'What've you got there?' asked Uncle Rufus.

'Love letter, is it? That sort of thing?'

Violet gave a quiet and gurgling moan that suggested romantic stirrings or chronic indigestion.

'It's not a love letter,' said Eustace. 'This was sent by an employment agency, inviting Percival to take a position at Bleakley Manor. Only, it wasn't a *real* employment agency. The letter was sent by the murderer.'

'And who the blazes was that?' demanded the Inspector, climbing angrily to his feet.

'The only person it could possibly be is the only person it couldn't possibly be,' said Eustace.

He left a carefully measured pause before he spoke again.

'It was Horton.'

There was a gasp from the assembled group.

Horton shook his head slowly. 'What utter nonsense, Master Eustace ... if you'll pardon me for saying so.'

The Inspector was now hopping on the spot. 'Gone daft in the head, have you?' he shouted. 'HE ... WAS

... LOCKED ... IN ... THE ... BLOOMIN' – sorry, m'ladyship – AIRTIGHT ... SILVER SAFE!'

'But it *wasn't* airtight, was it, Horton?' said Horatio. 'That's what I couldn't work out until Eustace explained it ... frightfully brainy bird, my brother. It should have been airtight, but it wasn't. There was never any danger of Horton suffocating inside.'

'The door of the safe was locked all right,' said Eustace. 'But there was plenty of air, and another way out, through a false back that connects with a secret passageway. Horton locked the safe door from outside after he drugged Cook, then – having scared the wits out of us with his Old Bramble Head disguise and taken advantage of the commotion to slip poison into Great Aunt Henrietta's glass – he used the passageway in Uncle Max's study to get back into the safe, ready for us to find him locked inside.'

There was a stunned silence.

'*Secret passages?*' scoffed the Inspector. 'Think I was born yesterday, do you?'

Sir Max lowered his head. 'Actually,' he murmured, 'there are secret tunnels all over the house. I discovered them when I was a boy.'

'Why didn't you let us all in on the secret, Max?' asked Uncle Rufus.

'Because,' said Loveday, 'he uses the passages to sneak from his study into his secret pickling laboratory without Aunt Maude finding out!'

'Oh, Max!' said Aunt Maude, her expression darkening. 'You promised.'

'I'm weak,' groaned Sir Max. 'The lure of pickling vinegar is too strong. I can't resist its siren song for a whole weekend.'

'It's not pickling we're investigating here,' interrupted the Inspector. 'It's murder!'

'Horton covered his tracks all right,' continued Eustace. 'He made sure that Percival was set up as the only possible murderer.'

'You shouldn't have kept the bill from the Stoat and Raven pub,' said Loveday, turning to Horton. 'That was a serious mistake. And the book on treasures of Ancient Egypt. You should always dispose of incriminating evidence.'

'What does the Stoat and Raven have to do with any of this?' asked Sir Max, lighting a cigar.

'It's where Watkins went the night he disappeared,' said Eustace. 'Horton was lying in wait for him. He abducted Watkins and then took his place.'

'This is too fantastical for words,' said Aunt Maude.

'No, it's all quite true,' said Horton, realising at last that the game was up. 'I can't deny it. They have described the events exactly as they occurred.'

A shocked hush descended on the room.

'But why *kill* Theodore?' asked Sir Max at last. 'Why not simply steal his wretched treasure, without having to murder him?'

'He would never have let that bust go ... the man was sitting on a fortune,' said Horton. 'He pretended he hadn't found the treasure, but the moment I set eyes on that terracotta bust in his room, wrapped up inside a big grey blanket, I knew exactly what it was.'

'First you tried to kill him with a snake,' said Loveday.

'Then a horrible great scorpion,' added Master Oliver Davenport.

Horton nodded. 'And when that didn't work ... well, you know the rest. That busybody, your Great Aunt Henrietta, was going to reveal the identity of the murderer – I heard her say as much in the kitchen before luncheon – so I made sure to get rid of her as well and make it look as though Percival had killed them both.'

A thought had been playing on Eustace's mind. 'Why did you go to all the trouble of trailing brambles around the Colonel and scattering the floor with blackberries?'

Horton smiled. 'I have always enjoyed amateur theatricals,' he replied. 'The prospect of conjuring up the spectre of Old Bramble Head at Michaelmas was too delicious to resist.'

Violet ran to Percival and flung her arms around his neck. 'Percy! My poor Percy,' she wailed, 'what's been done an awful wrong!'

Horton clapped his hands slowly and bowed to the children. 'I must congratulate you on your detective work.'

'What happened to Watkins?' asked Horatio, fearful that the faithful servant had met with a sticky end.

'He's quite safe,' said Horton. 'For now, at any rate.'

'You probably aren't even a bally butler!' ventured Uncle Rufus.

'On the contrary,' replied Horton with stiff dignity. 'I can assure you, sir, that I am indeed a butler.'

'Then why become a murdering sort of a butler?' demanded Sir Max.

'I've been turned this way by a lifetime of loyal service,' replied Horton. 'I was driven to desperate deeds by the masters and mistresses I've served.' He shuddered. 'The way they sip their soup. Vile. Disgusting.' He scowled at Sir Max. 'Not to mention the way they go on and on about pickles! It's enough to upset the strongest of stomachs.'

'And now you'll hang for your murderous ways,' said the Inspector. 'Your Michaelmas goose, as the proverb goes, is well and truly cooked.'

Horton smiled. 'I don't think so, somehow,' he said. He reached into the pocket of his tailcoat and pulled out a revolver.

'He's got a gun!' shrieked Aunt Maude. 'He's going to murder us all!'

Flinging the door open so violently that the hinges groaned, Horton made a break for it, running from the drawing room and along the hall, pursued by the children. Seizing the outstretched paw of the stuffed bear, he sent the creature crashing down on to the floor behind him to block their way. Reaching into one of the large Chinese vases, he pulled out a small golden statuette.

'The statue of Osiris!' shouted Master Oliver Davenport, as Horton fled through the front door, with Mustard and Pickle bounding at his heels. 'The treasure of Arn Akh. That's where he hid it!'

Outside, the wind had dropped to a whisper and

the island was wreathed in mist. Horatio was the first to reach the bottom of the stone steps, but there was no sign of Horton.

'Where did he go?' asked Eustace, running to catch up with his brother.

'I don't know,' said Horatio. 'Do you think he ran off into the marsh?'

The Bleakley family stood in baffled silence, gazing in vain into the depths of the thick, grey mist. Suddenly, the silence was broken by the guttural roar of an engine. Careering round the corner of the house came Uncle Rufus's open-topped sports car, with Horton at the wheel.

'Not my Borgstein Twin-Speed!' cried Uncle Rufus in dismay, as the car raced off in the direction of the road bridge, disappearing from view behind a tall box hedge.

'He can't get very far without the bridge!' cried Loveday.

The children ran on along the drive, with Inspector Hanwell and Uncle Rufus close behind. Rounding the box hedge they could see that up ahead the car had come to a halt.

'He's given up!' hooted Uncle Rufus. 'We've got the bounder now!'

But Horton had no intention of giving up. He revved the engine hard, the back wheels of the car spinning against the gravel. With a screech of gears the car lurched forward, accelerating quickly as it approached the splintered planks of the road bridge.

'He's going to try and jump it!' gasped Loveday, secretly admiring of Horton's pluck and bravado.

With a final sickening roar, the car bounced along the wooden planking and took flight into the mist.

Mustard and Pickle bounded on, barking furiously. The children raced to catch up, staring out across the flat marshland ahead.

'Did he make it across?' panted Eustace. 'I can hardly see my hand in front of my face!'

'Look!' shouted Horatio, pointing in front of him. 'There he is!'

Uncle Rufus howled as he followed Horatio's

finger and spotted his Borgstein Twin-Speed sinking slowly into the marsh. Horton had climbed out of his seat and was standing helplessly, clutching the golden statuette tightly in his arms. Crows circled high above him, cackling with diabolical delight at the man's unfortunate predicament.

'For pity's sake, help me!' cried the wayward butler, as the car sank deeper into the mire. Water was bubbling up from beneath, creeping across the bonnet. Soon Horton was up to his waist in the sucking mud.

There was nothing that could be done to save the man. The harder he fought to free himself, the more quickly he sank into the sticky and all-consuming mud. The children could only watch in respectful silence as he met his end. With one final and plaintive cry, the car and the butler were gone.

'How unfortunate,' said Master Oliver Davenport.

'Yes,' agreed Uncle Rufus sadly. 'I was frightfully attached to that little motor.'

Straining his eyes, Horatio could make out a strange

yellow light that seemed to bounce on the surface of the marsh. He held his breath, unaccountably anxious that Horton might re-emerge, transformed into Old Bramble Head himself. But as he stared ahead, the bow of a small boat broke through the mist. Standing at the front of the vessel, holding a flickering oil lantern in his hand, stood the unmistakeable figure of Watkins the butler. 'Look!' shouted Horatio, clapping Eustace so hard on the back that he almost sent his brother tilting headfirst into the marsh. 'It's Watkins! We've been saved!'

'Over to the right!' came Watkins' distant voice, as he turned to the two police constables who were acting as oarsmen on the vessel. Turning about, the constables rowed towards the very spot where Horton had disappeared. Leaning over the side carefully, Watkins picked out a small, glittering object, before it too could be sucked beneath the surface of the marsh.

'He's saved the treasure!' yelled Master Oliver Davenport, as Watkins held up the golden statuette and waved it triumphantly in the air.

By now the guests and staff of Bleakley Manor had all assembled at the edge of the marsh, waiting patiently for their rescuers to arrive.

'I was looking forward to them hanging you,' muttered the Inspector as he reluctantly released Percival from his shackles.

The footman rubbed his wrists and Violet squeezed his arm.

'No hard feelings?' said Eustace, turning and offering his hand to Inspector Hanwell.

But the Inspector glowered at the boy and thrust his hands deep into his pockets. 'Beginner's luck, that's all it was,' he muttered.

At last the rescue party reached the banks of the island and one of the police constables moored the boat to the branches of a half-submerged apple tree.

'There are bodies that need removing,' said Sir Max, bluntly. 'You'll find them in the ice house.'

'Oh, Mr Watkins!' cried Cook, as the butler stepped out on to dry land. 'It's a tonic to see you safe, and no mistake!'

Watkins was a grey-haired man of sixty, with a sombre face but a perpetual flicker of a smile playing at the corners of his mouth. He bowed his head to Sir Max, and presented him with the treasure of Arn Akh – the golden statue of Osiris, God of the Underworld.

'We thought you were done for,' said Horatio, hurrying towards Watkins and shaking the man warmly by the hand. 'However did you escape your captors?'

Watkins reached into his pocket and pulled out a crooked length of wire; it was an unfolded paperclip. 'As I taught you, Master Horatio,' he said. 'In case of dire emergency!'

The children related their story to the revered Watkins and he listened in silence, nodding his head at each twist and turn of the tale.

'It's like one of the murder mysteries that your Great Aunt Henrietta wrote,' said Watkins, when at last the story was told. 'The butler always did it.'

'That's it!' cried Eustace. 'B.A.D.I.! The Butler Always Did It!'

'So, all's well that ends well,' said Loveday, with a sigh of satisfaction, as the children made their way slowly along the drive and back to Bleakley Manor. 'Tomorrow, on my return to Miss Sunnybrook's School for tearaways and delinquents, I shall write the whole thing up for *Murder and Mayhem Magazine.* I'll send you a copy. I bet you sixpence you'll enjoy it. Or else!'

Master Oliver Davenport bit his lip. 'It didn't *all* end well,' he said. 'Some of it did, obviously. But, I mean to say, Horton *did* murder your uncle and great aunt.'

Horatio shrugged. 'No point crying over spilt milk,' he replied philosophically.

'Quite right,' agreed Eustace. 'It's probably as close to a happy ending as the Bleakleys are ever likely to get!'

The End

"A deliciously dark invitation to the strange world of Schwartzgarten." *We Love This Book*

OSBERT
THE AVENGER

Christopher William Hill

**ALSO AVAILABLE BY
CHRISTOPHER WILLIAM HILL**

TALES FROM SCHWARTZGARTEN

OSBERT
THE AVENGER

Read on for an extract...

CHAPTER ONE

——◆◆◆——

OSBERT **BRINKHOFF** was born on a Tuesday to a respectable family in an obscure corner of the city of Schwartzgarten. Mr and Mrs Brinkhoff, who had dreamed of rearing a genius, welcomed little Osbert's considerable breadth of skull and elevated forehead with undisguised glee.

'He has the head of an intellectual colossus,' observed Mr Brinkhoff.

'Indeed,' replied Doctor Zimmermann, eyeing the child with some suspicion as he packed away his forceps and stethoscope. 'I shouldn't be surprised if your little boy grows up to be the most intelligent citizen in the whole of this great city.'

And so it was that Osbert Brinkhoff's story began.

The Brinkhoff family lived in a comfortable apartment on Marshal Podovsky Street, close to the library and overlooking the greasy brown river that coiled like a serpent through the heart of Schwartzgarten. Mr Brinkhoff worked as a middle-ranking clerk at the Bank of Muller, Baum and Spink and had far more ambition for his son than he had ever had for himself. Even so, his own prospects were excellent, and it had been decided that when the ancient Mr Spink finally expired, the bank's name would be changed to Muller, Baum and Brinkhoff.

Mrs Brinkhoff was very proud of her husband, whom she adored. She would lie in bed at night and pray that Mr Muller and Mr Baum would die in a terrible accident, so that when Osbert was old enough he and Mr Brinkhoff could run the bank all by themselves.

But as the years passed and Osbert grew into a little boy, he showed no inclination towards banking. He was always small for his age, with pale skin and intense blue eyes. He had inherited his father's poor eyesight, and wore spectacles from his earliest years. He did not want to play with other children, but would instead sit for hours in his bedroom, reading books on physics and algebra that he had taken from his father's study, pushing a chair under the doorknob so that he would not be disturbed.

This was not quite the boy the Brinkhoffs had dreamt of. Finally, in desperation, they decided they had no choice but to engage the services of a nanny to look after Osbert, in the hope that she could prevent the boy from becoming irredeemably peculiar. Turning to the 'Home Help' section of *The Schwartzgarten Daily Examiner* on the eve of Osbert's sixth birthday, they found a small advertisement that seemed to answer their prayers: *Boys taken care of, no questions asked. Over thirty years' experience.*

On the day Nanny arrived, the sky turned a curious shade of mauve. The weather was warm and suffocating, and as Nanny hauled herself up the steps to the Brinkhoff apartment, Osbert watched her suspiciously from his bedroom window. Nanny was a large woman, almost spherical. She was dressed in black from head to toe: black boots, black skirt, black coat and black feathers sticking upright from her large black hat.

'Like an overfed raven,' thought Osbert, grimly.

Mr and Mrs Brinkhoff met with Nanny in the study and Osbert listened at the keyhole.

'You will find that Osbert is a very clever boy,' observed Mr Brinkhoff, the pride in his voice tinged with anxiety. 'But as with all clever boys, he must be watched very closely.'

The armchair in which Nanny sat groaned under her great weight as she leant forward, eyeing the Brinkhoffs with a steely gaze. 'The thing about boys,' she whispered mysteriously, 'even the oddest of them can become quite normal again. It's like gorillas in the zoo,' she rasped, and Mrs Brinkhoff coughed nervously. 'Little boys must be *tamed*.'

DON'T MISS THE TALES FROM SCHWARTZGARTEN SERIES